DARK CHILD

Dear Reader:

When I first started writing books, Travis Hunter was one of the first African-American authors who captured my attention. His vivid imagination and meticulous way with words has always fascinated me. When he self-published his first book, it was no surprise that it became a bestseller. It deserved it because it was so well written. Since then Travis has continued to engage readers in novel after novel, and it is a blessing to now be considered his publisher, and not merely his friend.

In *Dark Child*, we see a new and improved side of Travis' writing as he takes more risks and delves deeper into the psyche of his characters. The premise is strong and asks a serious question: when poor babies come up missing, who does care? Urban Brown is unforgettable. He is a man who has overcome the abuse and torment of his past and wants to live a normal life. But the actions of his desperate sister force him to engage in the struggles of those in his former community. So many people will be able to relate to this story. Many escape a type of hell but have to still deal with those who wish to drag them back down into the flames. Travis Hunter will make readers take pause and reflect, as they are overwhelmed by his words on the following pages.

Thank you for supporting Mr. Hunter's efforts and thank you for supporting one of the dozens of authors published under my imprint, Strebor Books. I try my best to bring you cutting-edge works of literature that will keep your attention and make you think long after you turn the last page.

Now sit back in your favorite chair or, better yet, chill in the bed, and be prepared to be tantalized by yet another great read.

Peace and Many Blessings,

Zane

Zane
Publisher
Strebor Books International
www.simonandschuster.com/streborbooks

ZANE PRESENTS

DARK CHILD

TRAVIS HUNTER

SBI

STREBOR BOOKS

NEW YORK   LONDON   TORONTO   SYDNEY

SBI

Strebor Books
P.O. Box 6505
Largo, MD 20792
http://www.streborbooks.com

ISBN 978-1-59309-245-0
ISBN 978-1-4165-9708-7 (ebook)
LCCN 2009924320

First Strebor Books trade paperback edition August 2011

Cover design: www.mariondesigns.com
Cover photograph: © Keith Saunders/Marion Designs
Author photograph: © McKenzie Dunn

10 9 8 7 6 5 4 3 2 1

Manufactured in the United States of America

For information regarding special discounts for bulk purchases,
please contact Simon & Schuster Special Sales at 1-866-506-1949
or business@simonandschuster.com

The Simon & Schuster Speakers Bureau can bring authors to your live event.
For more information or to book an event, contact the Simon & Schuster Speakers
Bureau at 1-866-248-3049 or visit our website at www.simonspeakers.com.

DEDICATION

The book is dedicated to the memory of my good friend,
Craig Grant

ACKNOWLEDGMENTS

I'd like to take a minute to thank a few folks who helped me through life as well as the writing process. First and foremost, I have to thank God for His continued blessings. Rashaad Hunter, my son, for making me smile every day. I cannot believe you are a teenager now, wow. My mother, Linda J. Hunter, for being the most supportive mom a guy could ask for. Monica Thaxton, thanks for my child. Carolyn B. Rogers, PhD. for your support and encouragement from the first day I ever decided to try my hand at this writing thing. Carrie Mae Moses just for being you' Sharon Capers, you are always solid as a rock; Andrea and David Gilmore, the coolest cousins in the South, Barry, Ray, Gervane, Ron, Lynette, Amado, Hunter, Tony (RIP); Louis Johnson, my dad. Ahmed Johnson, the best little bro a guy could ask for; Ayinde, Shani, and Jabadi. Dr. Clifton Johnson, Uncle Junior and Daryl Charles, Lester, Rhonda, Dallas, Dawson and Dylan Rivers, you know y'all my peeps. Jeff Cleveland for allowing me to whip you on the golf course while acting as my caddy. Clayton Jones, Jolette Law, Keneene Lewis, Ellis Sullivan, my potna; Errol Lampkin, thanks for all of the football talks, bro. Mary and Willard Jones, your support is remarkable. Pam and Ruffus Williams, you guys are solid as a rock. Sara Camilli, thanks for being a very good agent and not hanging up on me as I vented for hours about this crazy industry. Melody Guy, you still the bomb. Katrina Leonce, Linda Taylor and the Sisters Sippin' Tea. Moe Kelly, my brothers from a different mother, Eric Jerome Dickey and Jihad. Victoria C. Murray, Lolita Files, R.M. Johnson, E. Lynn Harris, Kim Roby, Kendra Norman Bellamy, Curtis Bunn, Colin Channer, Michele

Gibson and wonderful folks at *Written* Magazine, Sharon Guest, Shannon Holmes, Willie and Schnell Martin. Tammy, Lamont and Brandon Martin, Mark McClain, Monica (Imani) McCullough, Victor McGlothin, Tonya McNair, Sylvia Neysmith for the very first read of *Dark Child*; Trisha Thomas, can I be like you when I grow up? Brother Solomon Thomas-El, Zane; my young friend, Brandon Powe, keep doing your thing, little bro. And finally to the wonderful people of The Hearts of Men Foundation.

PART
I

1

"Get yo' hands in dem pockets, cracker," a deranged-looking man, who was obviously high on some form of narcotics, said while pointing a big silver pistol at his victim. "I gotta have it and you gonna give it to me."

The man's victim stood in front of him with his hands in his pockets. He seemed a bit startled but not to the point of panic. He surveyed the man with his eyes but never bothered to remove his hands.

"You deaf? Come out with the cash, cracker," the robber barked again, then stuck the gun closer to the man's face. "And I mean all of it. 'Cause I got places to be, gotdamn it."

A car turned onto the street, shining its lights on the robbery in progress, but the robber continued as if nothing was out of the ordinary. The victim, on the other hand, smiled. The car's lights allowed him to see something that instantly placed him at ease. Suddenly, this potentially life-threatening moment had turned into a somewhat amusing one.

The victim once had faced the barrel of a gun and he remembered being so scared he couldn't think straight, but not this time. One quick glance and he knew death's door wasn't in his immediate future.

He pulled his hands from his pockets and showed two clean palms. "Flat broke," he said with a smile.

The addict's eyes bulged as if they were going to fall out of their sockets. "You think I'm playing wit yo' ass, don't ya? You better reach again and come back with more than some damn lent," the robber warned. "I ain't no playtoy."

"I don't know what to tell ya," the victim said, turning his attention to the surrounding area of dark and grimy streets. He was in the heart of inner-city Atlanta and he couldn't wait to leave.

The robber placed the barrel of the gun at his victim's forehead and pulled back the hammer. "I...Ain't...Gonna...Tell...Yo'...Ass...No...Mo," he barked.

The victim was trying to locate his sister. Suddenly, the robber transformed from amusing to annoying. He pulled his head back and glared at the addict.

"You must be crazy. This is a gun, fool," the robber said, removing the pistol and shaking it in his victim's face. "Is you blind? Do you see this steel? I don't know if anybody ever told yo' ass, but guns kill."

"Go play with someone else, man," the victim said, trying to walk around the robber, but he was stopped when the gun was jammed into his back.

"Go play!" the robber asked, his voice rising a few octaves.

"I'm not going to ask you again," the victim said in a very low and serious tone.

The addict looked perplexed; he furrowed his brows and cocked his head to the side. "You the police?"

"No," the man said, turning around and facing his pitiful-looking nemesis.

"Don't lie, cracker, 'cause that's contrapment if you is. I know the gotdamn laws."

Urban Brown chuckled. As much as he wanted to destroy the man standing in front of him, he couldn't help but find him to be nothing short of hilarious. He shook his head and looked around again. This was not a social call and he wasn't trying to be out here all night.

"Why don't you just ask me if you can have a few dollars?" Urban asked.

"'Cause I don't want a few dollars, cracker. I want all the gotdamn dollars. And I know you the poooolice but I don't give a shit. Cop or not, I'm robbing yo' ass and I ain't telling you no mo."

Urban shook his head and took a deep breath.

"I gots places to be, where folks get high in the sky, baby," the robber said, taking a whiff of the high that would be forthcoming after Urban's money was in his possession. "You think I got all night to be out here robbing yo' preppy-looking ass?"

Urban actually laughed at that one.

"Oh, I see you think I'm Eddie Murphy, Chris Tucker, or some damn body. But let me tell you this, you simple-minded, cracker-ass cracker, I'll shoot the shit outta you."

This little game was getting old and the temperature was dropping by the second. Urban hunched his shoulders and pulled the fur on his coat a little closer around his neck in order to knock off the chill.

"Listen, man," the addict said in a frustrated tone, as if he were trying to reason with his victim. "I don't wanna shoot you. Lord knows, I ain't no killer, but I will. And check this out, if I shoot you, I'ma still rob you. I'm tryna help you. Damn, white people summa da dumbest muhfuckas I ever seen in my life."

"Allen Johannesburg Timmons," a voice shouted from about twenty feet away. "Whatchu doing, boy?"

"Damn it, Momma…" the addict snapped, turning his head toward the voice.

Urban used the distraction to his advantage and reached back and slapped Allen hard across his skinny face. The impact sounded like a gunshot and Allen fell back, holding his stinging face. He shook his head to clear the cobwebs, and then jerked the gun back toward Urban.

"Pull the trigger," Urban said. He was no longer smiling and was now stalking Allen. Allen was backing up as Urban reared back and smacked him again.

"You crazy? You better recognize who you dealing with, cracker. I'm the devil, gotdamn it!" Allen yelled, his voice cracking as the pain registered. "You don't slap me like I'm some bitch."

Urban slapped him again.

Allen yelled and pulled the trigger.

Click, click, click, click. The hammer hit an empty chamber over and over again.

"Momma," Allen called out to the skinny woman.

With no help coming from his mother, Allen reared back as if he were kin to Satchel Paige and threw the gun at Urban. The gun hit Urban in the chest and he caught it. He flipped open the revolver's cylinder, turned the gun, and showed Allen six empty chambers.

"Well, Mr. Devil, I'm going in here for about five minutes. Run and get yourself some bullets and try again," Urban said as he wiped away his prints with his sweater, dropped the gun to the ground, and then kicked it in the sewer.

He nodded respectfully at Allen's sickly looking mother, then turned and walked into the building behind him.

"Good thing you came 'round here when you did, Momma. I was about to kill a white man," Allen said. "Ain't no way I'ma let a white boy whup me. Shiiiiiit."

"I know that's right," his mother said. "But you did the right thing. You get prison time for fooling with white folks."

2

Three hours ago, Urban was resting comfortably on his California King bed with the sleep number set at thirty-five when the phone rang. He was tempted not to answer because he was in such a peaceful place, but the continued ringing shattered that state of mind to bits.

"Hello," he said in an incoherent tone. He was always a hard sleeper and it generally took him a minute or so to gather himself.

"Urban, you sleep?" a familiar voice said.

"I was."

"Well, get up," his foster mother's voice registered in his semi-conscious state. "Jamillah done lost her complete mind this time."

Upon hearing his sister's name, he was tempted to hang up the phone and go back to sleep, but the respect he had for the woman on the other end of the phone kept him talking.

Jamillah was Urban's younger sister and she happened to be strung out on any kind of illegal drug one could imagine. But to hear her tell it, she only had a nagging cold and was taking too much Robitussin.

"What did she do *this* time?" Urban said, lying on his back, trying to hold on to his sleep.

"She showed her little narrow behind up here with a baby. Baby couldn't be six months old and now she done up and disappeared. Now she can go out in the streets all she wants cause she's grown, but I ain't 'bout to let her have that baby out in this night air like that. It'll give him pneumonia and the whoopin' cough. She didn't even take the baby's bag with the milk and diapers in it. She showed up here without that. What the baby gone eat?"

Baby!

The mentioning of a baby got his attention. For as long as he could remember, he had a soft spot in his heart for kids, and babies were even more special to him.

Jamillah was a hot, ridiculous mess and he wanted no part of her, but if she had a baby and had him out there living in her world, then he had to do something about that. Besides, his foster mother's stress had always been his stress. The woman on the other end of the phone had raised many kids, but his number seemed to be number one on her speed dial list when things needed to be done.

"Call the police, Momma," he said.

"Lord Jesus, that Jamillah tryna kill me. My pressure already high and now she done ran out and did this," Wilma (Momma Winnie) Jackson said. "Why would she want to have that precious baby out in this weather?"

Momma Winnie had taken Urban and Jamillah in when no one else wanted them. Their biological parents were killed when Urban was thirteen and Jamillah was ten-years old.

Urban could picture Momma Winnie sitting on the side of her bed, wearing her tattered night dress, clutching a well-used Bible to her bosom, while praying to her God to deliver a person who wanted no part of deliverance.

"Why won't you call the police, Momma?" Urban asked again.

"Oh, boy, don't be like that. You know all they'll do is put her in jail and I can't stand to see nothing I raised behind no bars. That ain't no place for people."

"That's a good place for her."

"No, that's not a good place for her. She needs a little help; that's all. I've been trying to get her to go to church with me and let Reverend Power lay his mighty hands on her. You know he knows how to get them evil spirits out of her, but she won't ever stay round here long enough for me to get her over there."

Urban shook his head at his mother's foolish belief in a man who charged twenty dollars to heal someone by slapping them senseless. He could see the pastor and his hustling cronies sitting at a bar laughing at the pathetic memebers of his congregation who put their undying trust in his velvety words.

"Momma, that crap doesn't work."

"I ain't about to get into that with you this morning, boy. Now if you wanna stay a nonbeliever, then you'll have to answer for that on Judgment Day."

"I'm not a nonbeliever; I just don't believe in *that* fool. Anyway, did you give Jamillah any money?"

"I'm gonna pray for you, Urban."

"Thank you. It's always nice to know that you're appealing to the Man upstairs on my behalf."

"Boy, I don't know how the Devil done got such a hold on you. Good Jesus, I swear I don't know."

"The money, Momma," Urban repeated.

"No, I didn't give her any money and she didn't ask for none either."

"Did she steal any?"

"No, and I want you to stop being so doggone negative. I don't know why I even bother to call you," Momma Winnie said, fussing as usual. "You sho get on my nerves sometime with all that negative talk."

"Momma, go and check your purse."

"Urban, I don't need to go check nothing. That girl wouldn't steal from me. She said she was done with all that stealing and I believe her, even if you don't."

"She's done it before," he said as he stood and walked into the bathroom. He knew he wouldn't be getting back to sleep for a while.

"You need to learn to forgive. Read your bible sometime, 'Let he who is without sin cast the first stone,'" Momma Winnie said, quoting her favorite scripture.

"Momma, go and check your purse," Urban said, shaking his head.

Momma Winnie was as sweet as the day was long and was an eternal optimist but she was as naïve as a newborn when it came to the ways of a drug addict.

"Oh Lord, hold on," she said.

Urban could hear her mumbling about how foolish he was and how she was going to prove to him that Jamillah didn't take anything. The moan he heard in the background told him that the purse was a little lighter than it was before Jamillah had arrived.

"I'll go see if I can find the baby," he said when she came back to the phone.

"I can't believe she would go into my purse after I already told her how I feel about thieves," she said, genuinely hurt by her discovery.

"Get some rest, Momma. I'll check back in with you after I locate the nutcase," Urban said before hanging up the phone.

Urban walked into the bathroom, brushed his teeth, took a swish of Listerine, and washed his face. He walked into his spacious closet and got dressed. He had cussed his sister out so many times that he didn't even bother to waste his words this time. He couldn't count the number of times he had made the same trek out in the middle of the night, in search of his wayward sister after Momma Winnie called him crying. And yet, here he was again.

Urban drove around the areas in Southwest Atlanta where Jamillah was known to hang out. He scanned the streets as he drove at a snail's pace, hoping to catch a glimpse of her. These trips were always hard on him because he loved his sister with every fiber of his being; yet he hated what she had become.

Urban slowed down and started asking the people of the night if they had seen a scrawny, mix-raced woman who might be carrying a baby. Most of the natives looked at him as if he were a cop and had no words for him. He guessed it wasn't every day they saw a well-dressed white man riding around in the middle of the night asking about a drug addict.

Urban figured he needed a different plan of attack and started opening up his wallet as he asked the questions. Amazing! All of a sudden, folks had all kinds of Jamillah sightings. Urban had to marvel at the power of a ten-dollar bill with the folks who were considered have-nots.

After a few palms were greased, he used his power of deduction with the information he was given and figured he'd heard the "Ritz" too many times to ignore it.

"The Ritz Carlton?" he asked, confused, immediately wondering what in the world his sister would be doing at a high-priced hotel.

"Nah, brah," a short guy with about ten teardrops tattooed on his face said. "The Ritz Zoo." The short guy pointed to a warehouse behind them. "Roll up in there; you'll see what I mean."

Urban pulled his Chevy Tahoe in a space across the street from the ghetto Amsterdam and wondered what he was getting himself into. He reached into his glove compartment, removed his gun, a .40-caliber Glock pistol, and slid it into his coat pocket. It was three o'clock in the morning and he found himself walking into a scene right out of "Crackheads Gone Wild."

Urban crossed the threshold into the land of damnation. The second he entered the building, the odor of the place attacked his senses like a pack of rabid coyotes. He started to turn around but the thought of an innocent baby being exposed to this repugnance forced him to continue moving forward. He used his forearm to filter the disgusting aroma of drugs, urine, and human feces on top of unwashed bodies as he moved deeper into the crackhouse.

The scene before him was enough to drive a preacher wild and yet these people were up in there as if it were the new juke joint.

Urban stepped over bodies, empty beer bottles, and only God knew what else and winced time and again at the human destruction lying before him.

If there was a hell on earth, this had to be it. The only light illuminating the den of drug fiends came from a street post on the corner and the constant flicker of the addicts' cigarette lighters and matches.

"You wanna date, daddy," a girl, who sounded like she couldn't be any older than fifteen, said. "I'll suck yo' dick so good you'll wanna marry me."

Urban ignored her and kept moving. Fresh off of smacking some fool outside who tried to rob him without bullets, now he was fighting off women who were trying to sell him their polluted bodies.

"Hey, man," a baritone voiced man said. "She can't do it like me. I'll suck you better than that lil' skinny ho ever could. Give me ten dollars and I'll make you real happy, bro."

Urban frowned and fought the urge to vomit at the mere thought of the homosexual man touching him.

Nasty bastard! he thought as he stepped, then stumbled on what felt like someone's leg but found his footing. He looked down and saw a man sitting Indian-style while placing a needle into his arm, oblivious to all of the chaos surrounding him.

Damn, how can someone shoot up in the dark?

The place was so dark he could barely see his own hand in front of his face; yet he kept moving as he tried to get an eye on Jamillah.

This is some ridiculous shit, he thought.

Urban had always taken pride that he never stood in judgment of people, but he had to wonder, *How in the world could you let your life come to this?*

Just as he turned away from the guy on the floor, he heard a baby's cry. That had to be her. *God, please let that be her.* Urban changed his course and headed in the direction of the infant's cry.

The odor in the place was making him dizzy, so he abandoned the easy approach and started kicking, stepping on and over people as he made his way toward the window. People complained, cried, and threatened him, but he couldn't have cared less. The light from the street lamp was shining directly on Jamillah's haggard-looking face.

Urban stopped in his tracks.

Oh my God!

He hadn't seen his little sister in almost a year and a half and, even then, she looked horrible but now... Wow. She looked as if she were a walking dead woman.

Sweat poured from her paste-like face, even though the temperatures hovered in the low teens inside the dilapidated crackhouse.

The crying infant was squirming on the floor beside Jamillah while she held a crack pipe to her mouth and lit a flame.

Just as she was about to inhale, Urban stormed over and slapped the pipe out of her hand, knocking it to the floor and breaking it. Addicts nearby scurried like rats to retrieve unsmoked crack.

"Hey, hey, hey," Jamillah said, jumping to her feet with wild, bulging eyes. "Why you do that?"

Urban didn't respond.

One look at her and he could tell she was too far gone for any type of meaningful conversation. Urban reached down and picked up the baby.

"Oh hell to the nah," Jamillah cried, trying to grab her baby. "I need my money."

"He can't stay here," Urban said.

His voice registered with his baby sister and it stopped her in her tracks. She let go of the baby and placed her hands over her eyes to shield the light. "Urban?" Jamillah said.

"Jamillah." Urban's tone was nothing but business.

"What you doing here, big bro?"

"I came to smoke a little crack with you. Why do you think I'm here?" Urban said, walking away with the baby.

Jamillah quickly realized that this wasn't a social call and that her brother was leaving with the baby. She couldn't have that.

"Give me that baby and you go somewhere and mind your damn business, man," she said, grabbing at the baby.

Urban pushed her hand away from the baby, but she grabbed onto the child's tiny leg. He knew the fragile baby couldn't take her pulling on it so he reached out and pinched her ear.

"Ouch," she screamed, releasing the baby's leg. "Give me the baby, Urban."

"You should be happy I'm here to take her away from this…," Urban said as he looked around and couldn't even find the words for what he was seeing.

"It's a he and I got something set up. So mind your business. I got this," Jamillah said with a roll of her neck.

"Yeah, you look like you have everything under control."

"I do. These people gonna adopt him in the morning," she said. "They're giving me five-thousand dollars, Urban. Then I can get myself together. I know I look a mess but I'm telling you. This time it's gone be different. I'm ready to get my life together. Going to a rehab place; a real one. Not one of those bullshit places they send niggas to. I'm talking about one of those fancy spots. I got it all planned out. I'm about to get myself straight, big bro. You should be happy for me."

"I'm thrilled, but I don't know if anyone ever told you, you can't sell children. That's illegal."

"Man, these people gonna adopt him."

"That's not an adoption, that's a crime. Now move," Urban said, pushing her a little harder than he intended to.

"Fuck you and the law," Jamillah said, finding her balance. "I can do whatever I wanna do. Is the law gonna help me feed his lil' ass? Do you think the law is gonna buy some damn Pampers?"

"Where is his father?"

"Look around and pick somebody."

Urban couldn't understand how he could be surprised by her response, but he was. He frowned at what his little sister's life had become, then walked away.

"Hell to the nah," Jamillah said, walking as fast as she could in order to get in front of her brother. "The people gonna pick him up at eight o'clock in the morning. You can think what you wanna think, but he's gone," she continued, snapping her finger in his face. "In a few more hours, I'll be straight and he will too, so go on with your save-the-world ass."

"You are one sick individual and you should really seek some help. You know that?" he said, slapping her hand as hard as he could.

"Rape!" she screamed. "He's trying rape my baby."

"Shut up," Urban said and continued walking.

"You shut up and give me the baby. Now I need that money and I ain't about to let you fuck it up."

Urban walked around her, but drug addicts weren't known to give up easily when money was on the line. Jamillah reached out and grabbed her brother's arm, trying to stop him, but he just kept walking.

"Urban, please. Okay, I'll tell you the truth. I owe some people a few dollars and they want they money. They gonna hurt me bad if I don't pay 'em."

"I'ma hurt you if you don't get your hands offa me," Urban snapped.

She ignored him and kept talking.

"The people that I'm giving the baby to are real nice. They gonna give him a good home."

"Get your hands off of me," he snapped again with a low and deliberate growl.

"I can't," Jamillah cried. "Urban, please don't take the baby."

Urban was flabbergasted and heartbroken all at the same time. This person standing in front of him didn't look or sound anything like the beautiful little girl he used to know, the same little girl who couldn't go to sleep for three months after the death of their parents unless she was in his presence.

Her once pretty, cream-colored skin was now riddled with scars and pockmarks. Dark spots were all over her once beautiful face and that hair was a bird's nest of a mess.

"Jamillah," Urban said, stopping to face his sister. "I'll give you a thousand dollars tomorrow. After I give you this money, I don't ever want to see or hear from you again. I don't want to see you anywhere near Momma's house. Do you hear me? You can go and crawl in a hole and smoke all the crack you want."

Jamillah scratched her head and wrinkled her brows as if she were deep in thought. "I need it tonight."

"Tomorrow."

"Fuck you," she said, frowning up her bony little face. "Don't forget what I know."

"Don't *you* forget it," Urban snapped.

Jamillah looked at Urban with a mixture of fear and hatred burning in her eyes.

He walked around her and out the door. His nostrils welcomed the cool night's air and he took in a deep, lung-cleansing breath.

Jamillah was still trying to keep up.

"You gonna give me the money or I'ma call the police and mess up your perfect little world, Urban. I hate to do it, but I will. I still remember everything. You got a lot of nerve running around here passing judgment on people after what you did."

Urban paused and thought back to a rainy night fifteen years ago when he did something that changed his life and *him* forever. He forced the thought from his mind.

"I'm giving you one-thousand dollars. Take it or leave it," Urban said, not even dignifying her threat.

Jamillah started laughing. A very hearty, yet patronizing laugh.

"Five-thousand! If you want that baby, then the price is five-thousand dollars. And being that one little anonymous phone call from me to the proper people can shatter your little world, if I were you, I would get my banker on the phone as soon as possible, *big brother*."

Urban didn't respond; he just stared at the shell of a woman that stood in front of him.

"Yeah, you can mean mug me all you want, but tell me why I wouldn't use what I know to get what I need?" Jamillah asked with her bony hands on her hips.

"Momma Winnie's worried sick about you," he said, refusing to be baited by her.

That seemed to set her off. "Well, tell *your* momma I'm fine and stop all that fake shit. She don't care about me, you, or anybody else. Fuck her."

Urban couldn't tell if it was the drugs talking, but that response about the woman who cared more for her than she did for herself was way out of line.

"I should slap the taste out of your mouth for saying something that stupid," Urban said, feeling himself losing control of his temper by the second. "She's up right now, crying her eyes out over your sorry ass. She's probably the only person on this earth who still cares about you, you pathetic piece of shit. Now get the hell out of my face."

"Fuck you!" she screamed. "And you can tell your Momma I said to forget about me. Tell her you found me dead. Tell her I stuck a needle in my arm and blew my damn heart up."

"Why don't you go and make that happen for real!"

Jamillah got quiet and stared at her brother. She looked at Urban as his last words to her cut deeper than any other scar the streets could ever throw at her. She couldn't help but wonder if he really meant that or if he was speaking from anger. She needed to believe that it was the latter.

"What time will you be bringing me my money?" Jamillah asked as she fought the urge to cry.

"When I get up," he said, holding the baby close to his chest.

"What time, Urban?" she repeated. "And don't try to play me or you will regret the day you ever decided to play Mr. Badass, *big brother*."

Urban started walking again.

"I need some money. What do you have on you?"

Urban stopped, reached into his pocket, and pulled out two twenty-dollar bills. At that point, he simply wanted to get out of there. "Here," he said, holding the money out.

Jamillah snatched it before he could say another word.

It was time to leave the drug-infested neighborhood and get back to the comforts of his own life in suburban Atlanta. The baby was crying and he couldn't take the sight of Jamillah anymore.

Jamillah stuffed the money into her pocket. "Let's go," she said. A man who was lurking in the shadows joined her and they took off across the street. "I want my five-thousand dollars, Urban!" she yelled.

And just like that, she was gone.

Urban thought he was used to his sister's foolishness, but this took the cake. His heart broke into a million little pieces as he stared into the innocent eyes of the little brown-skinned baby.

Then he had a visual of Jamillah handing his nephew over to some crazed pedophile where torture and torment would be his only future.

Who else would buy a baby from a crackhead?

Urban looked at the baby and surmised he couldn't have been any more than a few months old. He was wrapped in a jean jacket and a dirty T-shirt served as his diaper.

"Let's go, little buddy," Urban said as they got into his truck. He blasted the heat. "Uncle Urban's gonna make it all right."

3

Jamillah crawled through a hole in the bottom of a door of an abandoned house. Her hands gripped the inside of the wood and she pulled the rest of her body inside. She stood and stepped across one of the filthiest floors one could ever imagine. However, to her it was a five-star hotel; it was far too cold to be sleeping outside. The place wouldn't be considered fit for a family of rodents; yet this was what she and her friend Marcus called home for now. She shivered and pulled her coat collar around her neck. The inside temperature seemed to be lower than that on the outside. Wintertime was always hard for her. Jamillah was a walking ball of fiery emotions. She was tired, afraid, angry, confused, and now that she thought about it, hungry. She felt around in the pitch blackness until her fingers touched the walls; then she led herself to what she thought was the center of the room. She walked toward the middle, reached up for the string that hung from the light, and pulled it.

Nothing!

"Damn you, Kenyé. You black bastard," she cursed the man whom she'd given a ten-dollar rock in exchange for him climbing up the utility pole out front to connect the electricity. "I'm so sick of these fools playing me like I'm weak. I'mma get me a gun and shoot somebody. Got me up here in the damn dark after I sucked his little ass dick," she fumed. There was still a small part of her that thought there should be honor in doing what you said you would do, even if she didn't always apply it to her own life.

Jamillah's stomach was roaring. She felt like her ribs were sticking to her back. Getting high was a twenty-four-hour-a-day job which left very little room for the necessities of life like eating.

Something smelled foul. She sniffed around and realized the smell was her. She took a whiff of herself and had to shake her head. "Damn, girl! You smell like something has crawled up in you and died," she said to herself. "I'll have to go to the gas station in the morning and get some of this funk off of me. This is ridiculous."

Her hunger pangs were coming down even more now that she had registered the thought. Cramps were kicking in and she wanted to cry. Her menstrual cycle was the last thing she needed and it seemed to be on the way. Damn it. She tried to remember the last time she had eaten anything, but couldn't. There was that box of crackers from two days ago. She jumped up, lit her cigarette lighter, and quickly scanned the room until she found the box of saltines. She ran to them and tore open the box, but it was empty.

"Damn you, Marcus," she cursed. "Selfish bastard. You know I hadn't eaten anything and you gonna go eat up all the damn crackers."

Jamillah found herself licking the plastic wrapper for any remains of salt or bread crumbs. She sighed, backed up against the wall, and slid down to the floor. A heavy sigh escaped her lips and she felt the weight of the world come crashing down on her.

Why me?

How long can I go on like this?

A tear rolled down her cheek as she thought about how far she had fallen.

Did Urban really mean what he said? Does he really hate me so much that he wishes I was dead?

How she wished for the days of old with her big brother. She missed their relationship and how he was such a fierce protector of her. The slightest threat from anyone, real or imagined, would send him completely over the edge. And as much as she tried to hate him, she would always love him for simply being him. She wished she would've called him when things first started getting out of hand with her life.

Jamillah was once a high school academic and athletic All-American. She had Division 1 schools sending recruiters as she was considered the next big thing. Universities from all four corners of the globe offered her scholarships for her exploits on the track and basketball court. After carefully considering all of the large and predominantly white schools, she felt an attraction to the historically black colleges. Maybe it was her father's words she heard in her head:

Know your history. Without that, you'll never know where you are going.

Jamillah chose Howard University in Washington, D.C. because she could kill two birds with one stone. She'd also had aspirations of becoming a lawyer who worked on Capitol Hill. Her father was very politically involved and obviously some of that had rubbed off on her. But little did she know, Washington, D.C. had other plans for her.

Jamillah stood in the long lines for registration. Her initiation to black college life, then began in earnest. When she wasn't in class, she was working out with the track team, and when she wasn't doing that, she was involved in some social club around the campus. She was fast becoming one of the most popular freshmen on campus. She was always invited to the "invitation only" parties and was always introduced to the campus's top people. In the land of pretty women and handsome men, Jamillah was considered to be the cream of the crop. So it was only fitting that she hooked up with the alpha male on campus, a high-yellow, city slicker named Rozon Harris.

Rozon was the quarterback of the football team, as well the campus's top party promoter. The buzz around school had already pegged him as the next Sean Combs, the famous entertainment mogul who once roamed the yards at Howard University.

Like most upperclassmen, Rozon was always on the prowl for a gullible freshman to add to his concubine. He didn't have to look far for the wide-eyed country girl who was totally enamored with city life. Jamillah was perfect for the picking. Rozon epitomized city life. He wore the finest clothes, drove a nice convertible BMW Six series, and had damn near every girl on campus changing panties twice a day. Jamillah felt like she had hit the lottery when he took an interest in her. Rozon had his own apartment, which made him seem more like a real man as opposed to the boys who were piled up in the dorms. And she floated on cloud nine when he walked across the campus to walk her to her class. All the girls envied her. Many of them gave her hateful and sly looks, but most of them wanted to know what Rozon was like in bed. That was a question she couldn't answer. She had no one to compare him to. Rozon was Jamillah's first sexual encounter, which made her fall even harder. She couldn't keep her mind off of him. The sex was amazing and all she wanted to do was be with him. Things were great her first year , but then, after the summer break, Rozon returned to school a different person. He stopped doing the parties and started hanging around a different set of friends. He quit the football team and a few weeks later, he dropped out of school altogether.

That should've been a big fat stop sign for Jamillah, but by then, she had fallen head over heels for the slickster. Rozon still maintained his apartment and kept up his top-model appearance, so she wasn't too put off or too overly concerned. But his new association with the roughnecks of Southeast D.C. raised her eyebrows.

Jamillah thought she needed to save her man from himself and wasn't about to bail out on him. After all, going through the rough times was all a part of being in love. She decided to go all out for him. She found herself competing for his attention. And he seemed to love her, but something else was quickly distracting him. Jamillah slowly but surely started fitting into his world, which meant she started doing whatever he was doing. All of her life she had stayed far away from alcohol and drugs, but now she found herself taking sips of wine coolers, then mixed drinks; then she starting puffing on a little weed.

Jamillah's track coach was the first to notice the change. She pulled Jamillah into her office and made her take a drug test. She failed it with a big "F." One month later, she failed another one and that was the final straw. She was kicked off of the team for the remainder of the year. Try as she might, she couldn't shake the urge to get high. She started acting strange and lost interest in school. She would stay with Rozon all day and all they would do was get high. Little did she know, her weed wasn't all natural cannabis; it was sprinkled with cocaine. She knew something was wrong when she smoked with other people and wasn't getting the same high she received when she smoked with Rozon. She approached him about it and he smiled. "That straight weed is for lames. That shit is a waste of money."

"But don't you think you should tell someone before you go mixing their stuff with coke?"

"Baby, if you don't like it, you can leave."

Those words were always so hurtful to her and whatever they were arguing about normally ended when he went there. She loved him and now that she wasn't on the track team anymore and wasn't staying in the athletic dorm, she really didn't have anywhere else to rest her head. Sure, she could've called Urban and he would've fixed her living situation, but then he would've wanted some answers as to why and how she got to where she was and she wasn't ready to go there. No, she would hang in there with her man and his laced weed.

It didn't take long for the money to run out and when the powder cocaine became too expensive, they downgraded. They needed the same high for less money so they found themselves running around Southeast D.C. looking for the rock man.

Jamillah wished she knew the crackhead's anthem, *One hit was too many and a thousand is not enough!*

Crack was euphoric.

Jamillah had never felt such a rush. The high was the best she had ever felt in her entire nineteen years on this earth. For the first time since she was a little girl, nothing mattered. No more haunting dreams stealing away her peace; no more worries about how she was going to tell her brother that she wasn't in school; no more worrying about what people thought of her. No more longing for her parents to return from their graves to love and raise her. The only thing that mattered was getting that potent crack smoke into her lungs and the wonderful feeling that followed. But little did she know the feeling would take her down a path of destruction that only God could alter.

Before long, Jamillah was doing all sorts of crazy things for money to feed her crack addiction. She had long forgotten about school. She moved in with Rozon and her body became their only source of income. Men and women had their way with her and she didn't care. Her mind was fixed on the feeling she would experience once the money exchanged hands for whatever deed they'd agreed upon. Sometimes she would think about how fast life comes at you and how quickly her life had changed from one that was filled with potential to one that was so low she felt as if she had already decomposed.

But then sex wasn't enough for some. Some fools wanted to get deviant. Her addiction trumped her morals and she became a slave to their desires. Some of the favors she did bothered her long after the high had evaporated, and as exhilarating as the crack smoke was, she still felt cheated. Slowly but surely, Jamillah started to feel less than human. One night, a nameless and faceless man gave her one hundred dollars to allow his German Shepherd to urinate on her. That was the night she sold her soul to the devil. Before crack, Jamillah used to attend church every Sunday and considered herself a child of God. But after crack and allowing herself to endure such humiliation, she didn't feel worthy enough to ever talk to God again. She was now one of Satin's angels.

Why me?

The question haunted her like an old evil spirit. Every time she thought she was on the track to beating the crack monkey, something or someone came to knock her back down, forcing her to wonder if God was so mad at her, that He was determined to keep her in the valley of the wicked.

4

Jamillah heard a rat scurry across the floor and didn't even bother to budge. She had gotten so used to living with lowlifes that the sound or sight of a rodent no longer affected her. The place she was sitting in had been home for the last week. It would only last another week or two before someone would come creeping around and force her to move to a different location. That is what all of her promise and potential had come to. But lately she had been thinking more and more about getting her life back together. She had tried numerous rehabilitation centers, but they were all a joke. However, she knew this couldn't be it. Something had to change and the years that she had spent living from pillar to post, robbing Peter to pay Paul the crack man, proved to her that nothing was going to change unless she changed it.

Damn you, Urban.

Urban had ruined everything. Guaranteed money and she was well on the way to making her plan a reality, but no, he had to come along and mess it all up.

She hoped he felt good about himself because he'd only helped to send her into a deeper hell than the one she was already living in. If she could, she would kill him. She thought seriously about killing her brother and wondered if she could really go through with it. After a few minutes of seeing his lifeless body in her mind, she quickly tossed the thought away. She loved him, even if he didn't love her anymore. But Momma Winnie was a bitch. She was being mean to Jamillah just for the sake of being mean and she would get even with her for that. All of that praying and crying and carrying on with her Bible was a put-on. Always down on her knees telling Jesus how messed up black folks were, and she was just as messed up. Jamillah would get even with her, if it was the last thing she did.

But, Urban...even though she wasn't going to kill him, he would also feel her wrath. It was because of him that she was broke, owed two different dealers, and would more than likely end up dead in an alley somewhere. The thought sent a streak of fear down her spine.

"Shut up, Jamillah. You ain't gonna do shit to Urban or Momma," she said to herself. "You need to get your act together. Look at you."

"You shut up," she answered back to herself. "I am getting it together. I'm tired of everybody telling me to get it together, including you, damn it."

This little back and forth happened a lot when she was high and out of her right mind.

And where the hell is Marcus? she wondered. *He'd better not be out there smoking.*

Before she could finish her thought, she heard a loud bump at the front of the house.

Jamillah tensed up. After all of these years on the streets, she still was afraid to be alone.

Someone was coming into the house and they weren't being quiet about it. There was a loud banging sound as if someone was trying to knock down the front door. She hoped it was Marcus, but why would he carry on like that? Something wasn't right. Marcus was a loner. She heard a voice, then a different one, but still nothing from Marcus.

She wanted to call out to him, but her intuition, or maybe it was a survival instinct, maybe both, were telling her to be quiet. She followed her inner voice.

"Why didn't you bring a flashlight?" the first voice she heard said.

"How was I supposed to know? Keep it down," the second voice said. "Okay, man, where is she?"

"I don't know if she's here yet, man," Marcus said. "I told y'all that already, man."

"Call her name."

"Millah," Marcus called out. "Millah, it's me. Where ya at, girl?" *Millah!*

Was that a sign? Marcus had never called her that. He was one of the few people who still called her by her given name. The folks in the hood shortened it because one more syllable obviously was too much work. She could also hear the stress in his voice.

Jamillah froze in place. She wasn't sure if she was even breathing. Something deep in her body was telling her that she was in a life-or-death situation. She wished Marcus would run away. For the first time in almost ten years, she prayed.

God, please let that fool run and whoever is with him, let them leave. If you help me, God, I will be at church on Sunday morning and I will stay until they kick me out. I know You don't believe me, but I'm for real this time.

Jamillah always had a very good feel for when things were going to go bad. She knew her parents were going to die on the day they died, and right now, she felt death around the corner from where she was sitting.

"She ain't here, man," Marcus said, with his high-pitched voice.

"Well, let's wait outside for her," the first voice said. "It stinks in here, man."

"You mind if I have my package now," Marcus asked.

"Here," the man said. "Don't you know smoking crack is bad for your health?"

Jamillah could hear one of the men laughing. He seemed evil.

"Yeah, but it's sure good to me," Marcus said. "And if I didn't tell you before, thank you very much for the smoke."

Jamillah wanted to smoke, too. She was tempted to come out and ask Marcus to pass the pipe, but her fear overruled her jones, so she stayed still.

"Let's get out of here, man," one of the men said.

"Shut your mouth, man. You just make sure you don't come with me again. You're more of a pain in the ass than these niggers."

"Hey," Marcus said. "White boys can't say 'nigger.'"

"Oh yeah," one of the men said. "Where is that written? And more importantly, what are you going to do to make me stop?"

There was the sound of metal on metal moving and clicking. Jamillah knew the sound of a gun when she heard one. She tensed up even more. Then she heard Marcus say, "Hey, man, whatchu doing? I helped you, like I said I would."

"No, you didn't. You said you were taking me to the baby. I don't see any baby. You hustled me and there is a heavy price to pay for doing that."

"Man, go ahead with all that. She ain't here yet. That's all. She's coming. We live here," Marcus said nervously.

"Yeah, I bet. Smoke up, nigger. Your presence and services are no longer needed," the man said.

"Come on, bro," Marcus said. Jamillah could hear him sucking on the pipe.

"I'm not your brother unless my father had jungle fever, and I highly doubt that," the man said. "But I'll tell you what I'll do. I will let you die high. So hurry up and finish your damn crack, loser."

"Please, man. Don't kill me," Marcus pleaded.

"Smoke up."

There was silence; then a loud bang vibrated the house.

Jamillah couldn't control her scream.

She jumped up and ran like she had never left the track field. She planted both feet and went straight through the glass window of the rear bedroom. She landed on the hard concrete outside the window. She made it to her feet, dazed and confused. She could feel blood easing down her face as she staggered down the alley.

The men up front heard the screams. "Go get her," the one with the evil voice said.

"No," the other one said. "Screw you."

Dazed, but still moving, Jamillah could feel her face swelling and more blood oozed down her neck. Then a big hand grabbed her and tossed her around. She looked into the freckled face of an orange-haired white man.

"Now is that any way to treat your house guest?" he said. Then he hit her on the top of her head with the butt of his gun.

5

Urban made it home around five-thirty in the morning. After leaving the land where the addicts roamed, he went to the twenty-four-hour Super Target in Buckhead. In the blink of an eye, he found himself fully submerged in parenthood. He carried his nephew in one arm while pushing the shopping cart with the other. Even though the little fellow couldn't have weighed more than twenty pounds, he got heavy real quick.

He made a bee line for the infants' department. All he expected to buy were a few items like diapers and milk. He ended up with a bassinet, a crib, a swing set, enough Pampers to last for months, about ten little onesies outfits, a car seat, baby wipes, a pacifier, and a case of Similac formula. Once the oversized orange cart was overflowing, he smiled. "You're already in your uncle's pockets, little man. How in the world are we gonna work this out?"

His little nephew looked up at him with sleepy eyes as Urban laid him on a display bed, cleaned him with a baby wipe, and changed him into a real Pamper. He found a little outfit and slipped it on him, too. Might as well do it all the way.

"May I help you, sir?" a lady wearing a red vest with Target Customer Service on the back asked him as she eyed him suspiciously.

"I'm going to pay for these things," he said. "It's a long story, but my sister is on drugs and I had to go get him..."

The lady waved him off. "Been there and done that. You go ahead and do what you have to do," she said peeking over at the baby. "He's a cute one."

"Thanks," Urban said and continued with his dressing. "Where are your coats that would fit him?"

The lady disappeared and returned with a little blue flannel outfit that had a hood attached. "This is all we have. They don't make coats that small."

"This will do. Thanks."

"No problem. See you at the register."

"I'm going to make it all better, little buddy," Urban said to his nephew after the woman had left. He looked to his left and saw the coolest little blue and white race car comforter for the baby's crib. He had to get it, so he tossed it atop all the other items. "That's it, dude. You will not send me to the poor house."

Daylight of the same morning, Urban was sitting in his living room assembling the baby's swing set when he heard the front door open. He jerked his head in the direction of the noise and felt his heart jump.

"Hey, babe," his fiancée, Sierra, said, as she placed her suitcase down.

He relaxed and jumped to his feet. He walked over and gave her a big hug.

"Hey, sexy lady," he returned.

Sierra had moved in two weeks ago and for the last week, had been on the road with her job. Urban was still trying to get used to her coming in unannounced.

Sierra stopped in her tracks as she took in all the new baby items scattered around the room. With wide eyes, she asked, "Did I miss something?" She stepped back from his embrace.

"Hey, baby," Urban said, looking down and rubbing his hands together. "I tried to call you, but I couldn't get through."

"Okay," Sierra said. "I'm here now."

"Well, I don't know how to tell you this, but...well..."

"Urban," Sierra said with a warning tone.

"Man," Urban blurted. "I had sex with these twins in Magic City and one of them got pregnant and they said it's mine but I don't remember which one I had..."

Sierra stepped back further. She stormed over to her bag and picked it up.

"Hey, hey, hey," Urban said, running after her. "I'm kidding. That's Jamillah's son." He wrapped his arms around her and gave her a nice squeeze. He could feel the apprehension in her body.

"Urban, don't get cute. What do you mean, that's Jamillah's son? When did she have a baby?"

"I don't know. Why didn't you answer your phone when I called you at five this morning?" he asked.

Sierra looked around and calmed down a little. "International flight, babe. Is she here?"

"Yeah, right," he said nonchalantly, sitting back down on the floor to continue assembling the baby's swing. "How was your trip?"

"It was alright," Sierra said, still amazed at what she was witnessing in their once tidy and quiet home. "So where is the baby?"

"In the bed. He finally went to sleep."

"He's here?" she asked excitedly. "What bed? How long has he been here? Where is he?" she wondered, walking into the bedroom.

"He's in the bed and please don't wake him up," Urban said, trying to take it all in stride.

Sierra came out of the room holding the baby. The minute he woke up, he started crying.

"You're just hardheaded, huh?" Urban said. "Now you figure out how to put him back to sleep."

"He is so adorable. My God, how old is he?"

"I don't know."

"What's his name?"

"I don't know that, either."

Sierra shook her head. "When did all of this happen?"

"A couple of hours ago."

Urban replayed the night's events with her and when he finished, she stood with an open mouth.

"Are you serious?" she asked.

"Yep. I couldn't leave the little fella there, so here we are," he said with a shrug of his shoulders. "He's already gotten me for all of my money at the Super Target. I didn't know they had so many things for babies. I got everything I thought he needed and still forgot a few things."

"Wow," Sierra said, stunned as she held the baby close. She had never really wanted kids, but holding this precious little child, who seemed so innocent and helpless, gave her second thoughts on motherhood.

"I don't even know if I'm feeding him the right stuff, but he devoured it. I need to get him to a pediatrician soon. Then..." he said, stopping to look up at his woman. "I don't know."

"My God. This is crazy," Sierra said, rubbing the baby cheeks with the tip of her index finger. "He is so precious. Oh my God."

"He has a set of lungs on him, I know that," Urban said. "I swear he's getting into the opera the minute he's old enough to talk."

"This world isn't right," Sierra said, shaking her head. "My sister has been trying to have a child for ten years. The adoption agencies are giving her the blues and she's spent almost a hundred grand on that fertilization crap, yet Jamillah is running around having babies and taking them to crack-houses. How insane is that?"

"You're telling me. Trying to sell a child for five-thousand dollars. She almost ripped his little leg off, trying to get him back from me."

"Wow," Sierra said, shaking her head. "Unbelievable."

"So it looks like I'm going to be an uncle with a live-in nephew. Are you okay with that?"

"Of course, man."

Sierra was thirty-two years old and already at the top of her profession as editor-in-chief of a major fitness magazine. She spent more time on airplanes and in hotels than she did at home. She had met Urban at an Anita Baker concert in Chastain Park three years ago. After the show, they went out for drinks. She had reservations about dating outside of her race, but Urban had never given race a second thought and treated everyone the same. He was one of the nicest men she had ever met, White or Black. He kissed her hand after the evening was over and made her promise to call him to make sure she had made it home.

The first thing the next morning, he called to invite her out to breakfast, which turned into an all-day talk. Urban shared with her his upbringing and all she could say was that he should write a book on all of his unique experiences. She was smitten with the tall white boy with the hood name. Six months to the date they met, they were on a sandy beach in Jamaica and he was down on one knee doing the corny proposal thing.

"You know my girlfriend, Raquel?" Sierra said.

"Yeah, the one with the big butt?"

"What are you doing looking at her butt?"

"Huh?" Urban said with a deer-in-the-headlights look on his face.

"Huh, hell," Sierra said, placing the baby down in his bassinet. "He is so adorable. Anyway, she's a pediatrician and I can give her a call."

"Cool."

"Why didn't you ask Jamillah the baby's name?"

"I was trying to get the boy out of a crackhouse. Pardon me for skipping the formalities," Urban said, looking at the swing set. "Something isn't right. I think I put these legs on backwards."

"Did you read the instructions?"

"I don't need instructions. It's only a swing."

"Yeah, it looks like you have it all covered," she said smartly, then turned to the baby. "Your Uncle Urban is going to have you breaking your neck. So we're not gonna put you in that swing until Auntie Sierra checks it out, okay? He'll be sleep soon," she whispered into the baby's ear.

"Whatever, I got this," Urban said.

"I know you do, babe."

The phone rang and Urban reached over to grab the cordless. "Good morning, Mother."

"You talk to your sister?"

"Yes, I spoke with her. I have the baby."

"Okay, what did she say?"

"She was high, Momma. Whatever she said wasn't very coherent."

"Well, how was she when you saw her?"

"She was worst than she was the last time I saw her but obviously she was healthy enough to still smoke crack. You should try to stop worrying about her."

"I'm not going to stop worrying about her. I'm not giving up on her. Where is the baby?"

"Right here."

"When are you bringing him home?"

Urban shook his head at the old girl's resolve. She had an in-house nurse due to a fall, which caused her to have a hip replacement. The doctor had her on about ten different medications for various ailments, yet she was trying to still take on the task of bringing up a newborn. Urban thought to himself, *if God ever created a better woman, He kept her for Himself.*

"Momma, aren't you tired of raising other people's kids?"

"I've raised forty-six kids in my seventy-nine years; one more won't hurt."

"That means you've done more than your share. Way more with some of 'em."

"Hush that fuss, boy. I live by the word of God and I thought you did, too. Read your Bible. Jesus walked…"

"Momma, Momma, Momma," he said, cutting her off before she got started on one of her long-winded Biblical tirades. "I need to get off the phone because I have to take the baby to the doctor. I'll call you later."

"After you get done, then you gonna bring him home?"

"I'll call you later."

Urban hung up the phone.

"Raquel said she can take a look at him before her first appointment. Can you get him over to Druid Hills or should I take him?" Sierra said.

"Nah, I'm sure you're exhausted from your trip. I'll take him. Get some rest."

"You are the sweetest man," Sierra said, leaning her five-foot-nine frame down to kiss him.

"Now that's true."

"And so modest."

"Not to mention horny," he said as he rubbed his hand up her leg.

"Nope, you gonna wake the baby," Sierra teased with a smile.

Urban turned his attention to the plasma television hanging over the fireplace. There was a roaring blaze. The newscaster was reporting that an abandoned building in Southwest Atlanta had burned to the ground and six people were confirmed dead. The building looked similar to the one the addicts called "The Ritz."

6

The doorbell rang as Urban fiddled away with his baby project. "Can you get that?" he asked.

"Are you expecting someone?" Sierra asked as she walked toward the front door.

"Nah," he said as he snuck a peek at the directions.

Sierra opened the door, then literally jumped back at what stood before her.

"Urban," Sierra said in a calm, yet frightened tone as she unconsciously backed up. "You'd better come here."

Urban looked at his woman, and after seeing a look of utter horror on her face, he jumped to his feet and raced to the door. What he saw shook him to his core. Not only did his sister look like the ghost of a dead crack-head and worse than she had a few hours ago, she appeared to have been beaten down. He took a deep breath, but stayed calm.

"Goddamn you, Urban," Jamillah said through clenched teeth.

Jamillah's face was battered and bruised almost past the point of recognition. A patch of hair was missing from the front of her head and the rest seemed to be matted in a brownish substance that appeared to be dried blood.

"What in the world happened to you?"

"I need to get the baby," Jamillah said, ignoring his question.

"What happened to you?" Urban asked again, genuinely concerned. He had to force himself not to grab her and pull her into the safety of his protection. But he had done that too many times and the protective layer he had for his sister was wearing very thin.

"You!" she screamed. "That's what happened to me, *you!* Now give me the damn baby. I told you those people weren't playing. Why couldn't you mind your business?" she said with her voice breaking. "Hunh? Why couldn't you just leave it alone?"

"Who did this to you?" he asked again in a firm, businesslike voice.

"Can you go and get my baby, please?" Jamillah pleaded, slowly and deliberately.

Urban could see that his sister was a ball of emotions. She looked scared, and totally confused. She also appeared to be as high as a kite.

"Jamillah," Sierra said from behind Urban, "would you like me to take you to see a doctor?"

"Hell no!" she snapped. "I need for you to take me to see my damn baby!" she screamed. "And I don't have all damn day!"

"Calm down," Urban said.

"Screw you, man. You need to go get that baby before I call the police and tell them you kidnapped him."

"Would you like to use my phone?" Urban said. "Because I would love to see what kind of police officer would release a child to you in your condition."

"Just go and get the baby," Jamillah said, abandoning her threat.

"No," Urban said. "Now you're more than welcomed to come in here, clean yourself up, and tell me what's going on. I won't let anything happen to you."

"The baby, Urban. Go and get the baby," she snapped.

"You wait right there," Urban said, closing the door and locking it behind him.

"Please tell me that you're not about to give her the baby," Sierra said the second he turned around.

"No, but I told her I would give her some money. I'm thinking the people who beat her down are the same ones she owes. So I can probably get her a little relief, but knowing her, she'll be right back in this same predicament next month, or maybe even next week."

"How much money are you giving her?"

"A grand. After that, she's on her own."

Sierra gave a confused glare, then it turned into a snarl. One of those *how could you be so cold* snarls.

"What?" Urban asked.

"That's your sister, Urban! Don't you even care a little bit? I mean, she's out there on our front porch losing whatever mind she has left, and all you can do is stand here and judge her. You're her older brother; you're supposed to look after her."

Urban paused and stared at the woman he'd said he wanted to spend the rest of his life with; he realized this was a test. They had never really disagreed on anything of any real relevance.

He took a deep breath and nodded.

"You're right. Why don't we help her? You still have your townhouse in Buckhead. Why don't you let her stay there? I'll take over the payments for as long as she's there."

Sierra paused and narrowed her eyes at him.

"What's the problem? You live here, right? Nobody is staying there. It's a very nice place, yet it's empty. I think Jamillah would really enjoy cleaning herself up in that big Jacuzzi bathtub. The only thing is, she won't clean herself up. She'll sell everything in there. She'll have crackheads running around your place like it's a party and once it's all fucked up, she'll move on like nothing ever happened. I can't let her stay here. I have to work. And I'll be damned if I come home to an empty house because she found a soft heart to prey on. Been there, done that. So you wanna try your place?"

"That's not fair."

"Why? You and I are getting married. So that makes her your family, too. The economy is jacked up so nobody is buying houses right now. Why don't we let her stay there?"

Urban could literally see Sierra's temperature rising.

"You and I have been together for what? Almost three years. Jamillah has been on drugs for damn near ten years. Did you ever think for one second that this is not our first go-round with this crap? Do you think that I might've helped her out a time or two or three or four? Maybe five or six, seven or eight. Hell, I've lost count of the times I've seen this scene," Urban said, his voice rising as he felt his own temperature rise. "Have you ever thought about that?"

"Maybe you have, but obviously it wasn't enough."

"I've done enough," he said, shaking his head. "And all that I'm going to do."

"I don't know if you've done everything you could. Why don't you enlighten me?" she said and placed a hand on her hip.

"Enlighten you?" Urban said, not believing what he was hearing. "I almost said something to you just now."

"Say it."

"Why don't you leave this alone, because you have no idea what you're talking about."

"Maybe I don't, so why don't you get me up to speed," Sierra said. "I want you to explain to me what kind of man would leave his sister, who looks like somebody beat the hell out of her, out on the steps in the cold. What kind of man would do such a thing?"

Urban felt himself losing it. How in the world could she stand there and demand answers? Who was she for him to answer to?

"I've been looking after her for years; it's time she looks after herself," he said calmly.

"It doesn't appear to me like she can look after herself, Urban," Sierra snapped.

"Sierra, leave it alone."

"No. I will not leave it alone and I will not stand here and allow you to take her baby and treat her like she's not even a human being."

"LEAVE. IT. THE. FUCK. ALONE!" Urban finally lost his cool.

"Who are you talking to?" Sierra's face frowned as if she had been bitten by a snake.

"I'm talking to you," Urban came back at her.

"No, you're not."

"Listen, this thing has been going on way before you, and if you don't learn how to mind your business, it'll still be going on after you."

"So what are you saying?"

"I'm saying if you don't respect my wishes for you to stay out of this, then you can get the hell out."

Shock registered on her face, then it quickly turned to anger. "Oh, this will be the last time you ever tell me that," Sierra said as she turned on her heel and marched into the bedroom closet. She started snatching clothes from their hangers. "I don't need you. I'm not some desperate broad who can't do without you. You're not going to talk to me any old kind of way under any circumstance. Who in the hell do you think you are? You must have been smoking some of that crack your sister is on, if you think I'm the one. No, sir. If you'll treat your sister like this, then there is no telling how you'll treat me. But I see your true colors," Sierra rambled.

Urban ignored her and walked into his own closet. He pulled back a layer of carpet, removed a faux piece of wood, then placed his finger on the scanner and the safe chimed and opened. He pushed past his passport and a few pieces of high-priced jewelry and snatched a thick wad of cash. There had to be at least fifty thousand dollars in there. He peeled off ten hundred-dollar bills, tossed the rest back in, closed the safe and replaced the wood, then the carpet.

When he walked back into the living quarters, Sierra was still on her verbal rampage.

"I'll be damned if I work as hard as I do to come home to this. Asked you a simple question…" Sierra rambled.

He wasn't listening to her anymore. That was how he was; he dealt with the task at hand. Sierra was free to leave and if he never saw her again, it would be okay with him. Sure he would be hurt, he loved her, but he would get over it. His life had been filled with losing loved ones and he had learned never to get so close to a person that you couldn't do without.

His mind was on Jamillah and what was really going on with her. He had to admit that he had never seen her this low. She was a mess, but never had it gotten to the point of her being assaulted. And as much as he despised her drug abuse and subsequent trifling behavior, she was still his sister and he didn't appreciate anyone beating her ass. On the other hand, if she was running around stealing from people to feed her habit, then she had gotten what she deserved. He vacillated a little with his thoughts and then opened the door.

7

Jamillah wasn't on the porch where he had left her. Urban stepped out onto the porch and peered down the street. He saw Jamillah standing by the passenger door of a navy-blue Crown Victoria. When Jamillah saw Urban, she pointed at him and then nodded her head. She dropped her head, then said something to the man and hurried back to his yard.

"Where's the baby?" she asked, running up to Urban.

"Who is that?" he asked, nodding at the car.

"My ride."

Something didn't seem right. Dealers didn't give crackheads rides. And from what he could make out from his vantage point, those guys didn't seem like dealers; at least not street-level ones.

"Your ride?" he said, eyeing the occupants of the car.

"Where is the baby?" she asked anxiously. "Come on, Urban, this isn't a joke."

"Here," he said, handing her the money, but still checking out the car.

She snatched the money from his hand and stuffed it in her pocket. "I need the baby, Urban, for real."

Urban took his eyes off the car and bore into her. "You are not getting that baby. Now whatever kind of sadistic shit you have going on with those clowns is your business, but you will not get that baby."

"Urban, if you don't give me that baby, then I'm as good as dead."

"Well then, that's how it has to be. That's the bed you made," he said. "May you rest in peace in it."

The look on Jamillah's face said that his words had hurt her more than those men's fists ever could.

"You have a nice day," Urban said.

"Urban, give me that damn baby!" she screamed. "They gonna kill me."

Urban stopped and turned around. He stared at his baby sister. She was raggedy, dirty, battered and bruised and he wondered what had happened to his favorite person in the entire world. He missed the little girl she used to be. He missed her so much that if he were given a guarantee that she would be okay if he gave his life, he would stand in front of a firing squad without a second thought. But that wasn't the case. He felt himself tearing up. They were as close as two people could ever be, but the drugs had taken his place. The drugs had robbed them of the bond they had shared through so many challenging days and nights. Crack was her brother now. She had buried Urban long ago when she took her first hit, and placed him into a deeper hole with each subsequent toke of the glass idol she worshiped. Urban dropped his head.

"They will kill me, Urban," she pleaded, tears streaming down her face.

Urban quickly wiped away his own tears as he realized that death might be a welcomed reprieve from what she had become. "You're already dead," Urban said as he wiped away the tears.

Jamillah's pitiful look changed in an instant as if she suddenly realized getting the baby wasn't an option and she had to get to plan B in a hurry. She took one look at the car with the white men sitting in it and took off running in the opposite direction.

"Fuck you, Urban!" she yelled as she ran like a track star toward the back of his subdivision.

The men in the car didn't give chase. Instead, they eased out into the street, pulled in Urban's driveway, then backed up and drove off.

Two white men, dressed in crisp white shirts and shades. One of them even nodded at him.

Interesting!

8

Jamillah was running. She had visions of being on the track at Howard as the crowd of ten thousand cheered her on in Greene Stadium. Her dirty Nikes hit the pavement with the ease of a gazelle. After all of these years, she still ran with the grace of Marion Jones. She had no idea where she was going but she knew she needed to get there fast. Her life was now in grave danger but all she could think about was revenge against her brother and foster mother for putting her in this position. She wanted to kill both of them so badly that she couldn't think straight.

Jamillah looked around the area as she ran. Her mind raced as fast as her feet were moving. She couldn't think of anything. She was a fish out of water. Surrounded by fancy cars and rich white people, all of them seeming to be on the positive side of wealthy, she was on the negative side of poor—slap dead in the middle of their world.

The people she passed looked at her with disdain. She hated them, too. She caught a glimpse of an old white woman standing on her expensively manicured lawn with what had to be the ugliest dog in the world. But how she wished she could trade places with her. The white lady pulled her dog close to her and literally ran to her house as if the mere sight of Jamillah was going to send her into cardiac arrest.

What the hell are you running for, bitch? Jamillah thought as she kept dashing. She hated herself for getting that reaction but hated the woman even more for giving it to her.

Her mind shifted back to those men. *Why were they so angry? Was getting a baby that important?* She wondered as she ran.

Marcus was dead.

They had killed Marcus.

Why did they kill Marcus?

Her eyes started watering again. Marcus was a good guy. He could've never hurt a soul and as much as she'd allowed herself to do so, she'd loved him. He didn't have anything to do with the deal she'd made with those people for the baby and yet he had died for it.

Jamillah tried to block everything from her mind and concentrate on the here and now. Her legs were beginning to ache and her lungs were threatening to explode. She slowed her sprint to a fast trot and instinctively held her hands above her head. She kept looking around for the evil and murderous men but they were nowhere to be found.

She thought about the money Urban had given her and instantly felt hunger pangs. Fear had a strong hold on her, but hunger was quickly stealing her attention. She exited the subdivision and raced across the busy four-lane highway and into the parking lot of a Quick Trip gas station. She walked into the store and caught the attention of the two customers who were roaming around. They gave her the same look the white woman had given her, but she ignored them and went straight for the deli section. She took two sausages from the grill and removed two buns from the heater. She added a little mustard, onions, and chili to both of them and grabbed a bag of potato chips. She grabbed a twenty-ounce Sprite and walked to the counter. The clerk eyed her suspiciously but she ignored him and placed the items down.

"Those sausages are…" he paused, taking in the sight of her horrible-looking condition. He could not hide the surprise on his face. "Those sausages are not two for a dollar," he said rudely.

"I didn't ask you that," Jamillah snapped.

He seemed stunned by the response and tried to recover.

"I know, but people come in here all the time and get it mixed up," he explained, adding a smile. "Didn't want to surprise you when I rang it up."

Jamillah ignored him and stood there. The guy took the hint and started ringing up her items.

"Seven dollars and thirty cents," he said.

Jamillah pulled out one of the hundred-dollar bills Urban had given her and handed it to him. She looked around for a restroom as she waited for her change.

"Where is your restroom?"

"Outside, behind the building."

"Thank you."

Once she had her change, Jamillah walked around to the back of the building where she found the restrooms. She needed to get herself cleaned up, but she couldn't see herself taking her food into a nasty bathroom. It was funny how her habit had her living in some of the worst conditions known to man, yet she never could allow herself to take food into a bathroom. Jamillah stopped and sat on the sidewalk by the restroom. She opened her drink and took a big swallow. Next she opened up one of her sausage dogs and almost devoured it with one bite. The smell alone sent a soothing comfort throughout her body. She took a big bite of the second one and savored the taste of her first hot meal in at least a week.

As she enjoyed her food she looked around for a MARTA bus sign. She looked out into the busy intersection and didn't see any form of public transportation. "Damn," she said. "How in the hell am I going to get out of here?"

She was stuck in suburbia without a crackhouse in sight. What was she going to do with herself?

9

Biopp, biopp, a police siren blurted and startled Jamillah.

A gray and black cruiser pulled up directly in front of her and a short Mexican police officer got out of the car. He walked over to Jamillah and did a double-take at her condition.

"Ma'am," the young officer asked, "are you okay?"

"Yes," Jamillah said as she quickly chomped down on another bite of her sandwich before gathering her chips and drink. She stood and started walking away.

"Are you lost?" the officer asked, walking behind her.

"No," she said and continued walking.

"Stop," the officer ordered.

Jamillah thought about running but her legs wouldn't cooperate. She was tired and her body was starting to feel the effects from the beating she had received from the evil white men.

"Ma'am, could you please come back over here for a minute," the officer said in what was more of a command than a question.

Jamillah wanted to run but figured she was in a no-win situation. Aside from being a fashion misfit in an affluent area, she really hadn't done anything.

"You look like you could use an ambulance. Would you like for me to get you one?" the officer asked.

"No."

The officer walked over and stood in front of her.

Jamillah had to force her knees from shaking as she stood. She hated the police. The guys in blue and her kind were natural enemies, no different than a lion and a hyena. But when she looked at the man standing before her, she found him unlike other officers. Something in his eyes said he was compassionate.

"Ma'am, do you have any identification?"

"No."

"What's your name?"

"Jane Doe."

"Okay," the officer said with a disappointed look that said she wasn't going to make this easy. "May I ask where you're coming from?"

"My brother's house," she said in a low tone as her heart rate increased.

"What's your brother's name?"

"John Doe."

"Where does Mr. John Doe live?"

Jamillah turned around and pointed in the direction where she had come from. "Hey, I'm not bothering anyone. Can I go now?"

"Ma'am, you have blood all over your face and a nasty gash under your eye. You mind telling me how that happened?"

"I fell."

"Ma'am, I'm going to call you a medic. After they check you out, then you'll be free to leave."

Jamillah looked at his gun. She wondered if she could grab it, shoot him, steal his car, drive back over to Urban's house, shoot him, too, and then take the baby.

The officer said something into the radio handset that hung from his shoulder.

"Would you like to have a seat, ma'am?"

"No," she said. "Can I go?"

"No, ma'am. The paramedics will be here in a few minutes. You can sit down and finish eating if you like."

Jamillah sighed. She realized there was no way out, and she also knew that her body was in desperate need of medical attention. She felt as if she might have had a broken rib or something.

"Thank you," she said, surprising herself by accepting the offer.

The officer opened the passenger door for her and she walked over and sat down.

"So you say your brother lives around here. Did you guys get in a fight?"

"No, he hates me but he wouldn't hit me."

"Why does he hate you?"

Jamillah held her arms out wide. "Why do you think?"

"I don't know," he said.

"Because I'm …" her voice drifted off. "Because I'm a loser. Because I'm addicted to drugs and can't seem to kick the habit. Because I'm a disappointment to him. Should I go on or do you get the picture?"

"Being a loser is a state of mind and you can kick the drug habit anytime you want, but you have to want it," he said with a slight smile.

"I've been an addict for a long time. I'm addicted to crack cocaine. He wants nothing to do with me. He told me I was dead to him," she said, fighting back the tears as the thought of how her brother felt stabbed her deep inside.

"I see," the officer said. "I can get you some help if you like."

"Been there, done that and got a thousand T-shirts to prove it. The rehab centers are a joke," Jamillah said, then all of a sudden felt bad for treating the officer so rudely. He seemed to be a very nice guy who genuinely wanted to help her. He was a far cry from the City of Atlanta police officers, who seemed to take great joy in mistreating the unfortunate by beating them up even more than they already were.

But this was Dunwoody and the cops seemed to be different. Or did she just get a good one? Either way she felt blessed to be in the man's presence. She really needed some kindness in her life and he was exactly what the doctor ordered.

"Well, most places are what you make them," the officer said. "May I give you my card? When you're ready, I can help you get yourself checked into one. You seem like a bright woman."

"I *was* a bright woman, but bright people don't make dumb decisions that cost people their lives," she said with tears flowing again.

"Whose life are you talking about?"

"Everyone who loves me," Jamillah said, realizing she was talking to a cop. "They are all dead to me. And I'm dead to them."

"It doesn't have to be that way. Here," the officer said, handing her the card.

Jamillah looked at the card. Then she got the brightest idea she'd had in a long time.

"You're a nice man," she said, looking at the card. "Officer Juan Vargas."

"Thank you. And you seem like a nice woman. You'll be an even nicer one, once you get yourself back on track, and I'm sure you can bring all those dead people back to life."

"That is very nice of you to say. You seem pretty sure that I'll get back on track. Obviously you don't know me very well."

"I have the gift of discernment," he said, smiling with perfect teeth. "And you can do great things when you put your mind to it. Maybe this is life's way of preparing you for the great things you will do."

"Laying it on a little thick, don't you think, Officer Vargas?"

"I'm only being honest. The first step to recovery is to believe it can happen," Vargas said with a smile.

Jamillah nodded.

His smile reminded her of her own raggedy mouth and she became sad again.

"Where is this rehab place you're talking about?"

"There are several, but we can get you to one that's close to your home. That way, your family can come and support you."

"No," Jamillah said, shaking her head. "I want to go to the one farthest away from them. If I'm going to do this, that's the only way I'll do it."

"It's always easier when you have a support system," Officer Vargas said.

"I have to do this alone. If not, then it was nice knowing you," she said, getting up.

"No, no, no," Vargas said, holding out his hands. "Look," he said, pointing at the ambulance that had pulled up. "It must be your destiny."

Jamillah huffed and stood. She walked over to the ambulance and was approached by two young medics who reached out to her as if she were about to fall. They led her to the back of the van and sat her down.

"You're definitely going to need stitches," one of them said, running his fingers across a nasty gash in her head. "My God, what happened to you?"

"I fell," Jamillah said with a sarcastic smirk.

"Are you having trouble breathing?" the other medic asked.

"Yes," Jamillah said honestly.

After a few more pokes and prods, the medic suggested they take her to Northside Hospital for admittance.

Jamillah's first thought was that she couldn't imagine sitting in the hospital for any amount of time. The money Urban had given her was itching to get to the dealer so she could smoke her troubles away. But then she thought about those men. That's when she realized there couldn't be a better place to rest and rethink.

She could care less about rehabilitation or getting whatever was poking her insides fixed. What she needed was a hiding place because those evil men wouldn't be so kind to her the next time. That much she knew.

10

Urban sat in his favorite chair while cradling his nephew in his arms. *SportsCenter* played on the plasma screen hanging over the fireplace, but his mind was moving a million miles an hour. He was wondering how he was going to deal with this latest crisis that Jamillah had created.

Urban took great pride in his ability to have all the answers, at least when it came to his life. He always tried to keep things real simple, work hard, and never get too caught up in anyone or anything—ever. But life was throwing him curve balls that he couldn't catch up to. This Sierra business was weighing heavily on his mind and that alone was unlike him. The minute a woman showed signs of drama, he mentally checked them out of his brain. But this time, his mental library kept returning an item he wanted out. Even though he felt Sierra had crossed the line, something inside of him wanted to talk to her, fill her in on his past so that maybe she would understand.

Try as he might, he couldn't keep his mind off of that woman. He had picked up the phone to call her at least fifty times, but couldn't dial the numbers. In the past, when relationships went awry, he never thought twice about dialing their digits. But now he spent so much time wondering how she was doing, if she were thinking about him. He reached over and picked up the phone, dialed her number, and hit "call." The phone rang three times, then went to her voicemail.

"Hi, this is Urban. I want to apologize about the way I acted last week or was it the week before last? Seems I haven't slept since the little fella got here. Anyway, I am sorry. If you feel like talking, then give me a call. If not, I understand," he said before hitting the "end" key on his phone.

Urban ran his finger across his nephew's forehead, which always seemed to make the little guy smile.

"Man, what am I going to call you? I gotta get you a name. I can't keep calling you 'the little guy.' What do you like?" he asked with a smile. "What about Brandon? I like Brandon and you look like a Brandon. So Brandon it is. Brandon Brown." Urban took the tiny hand into his and shook it. "Nice to meet you, Brandon Brown. Nah, let's go with William. I like William better. My father's name was Willie so we'll give you the smoother version. Yeah, I like William much better."

Urban ran his long fingers through his curly hair and took a deep, stress-relieving sigh. His eyes spotted a framed photo of family. In the picture, they were at Six Flags and all smiles. Who could've ever guessed that three hours after that picture was taken, his life would be changed forever?

"How long before we get home," a nine-year-old Jamillah whined. They were headed back to their home in Augusta, Georgia, which was almost a three-hour drive from Atlanta.

It was 1988 and the sight of a black man, a white woman, a white, curly-headed boy and an interracial little girl, still caused lots of hateful stares. But their mother, Maryland Brown, could have care less what other people thought. She was her own woman and she had found the perfect soul mate in Willie Brown, a hard-working man, who worked even harder to provide for his family. Despite growing up in a small Southern town, where racism was rampant, Willie never gave it any power. To him, people were people. You could find good ones and bad ones of all ethnic groups. Where he grew up, most of those bad ones were White, but he had met enough good ones to keep him open-minded.

"A hundred more hours," Willie Brown, Jamillah's biological father and the only man Urban ever knew as his dad, said with a smile.

"How long is that?" Jamillah asked.

"Count to thirty-six thousand by ones," Urban said. "Real quiet."

"Daddy, tell Urban to leave me alone."

"Urban, leave your sister alone," Willie said with a wink through the rear view mirror.

"I'm trying to keep her busy, Dad," twelve-year-old Urban said with a smile. "You know how she gets restless on long trips and keeps asking over and over and over and over…"

"Oh hush, Urban, you're not much better." Maryland Brown defended her daughter.

Willie gave Urban that male secret look that said, *women.*

"Let's sing a song," Maryland suggested. Nothing made her happier than being with her family and it showed with everything she did.

"I ain't no joke, I used to let the mike smoke, but now I slam it when I'm singing, to make sure it's broke," Urban yelled at the top of his lungs. "Cause when I'm gone on one good song…"

"No sir, no sir, no sir," Maryland interrupted her son, shaking her head. "No rap. That is not music. I don't know what it is, but it's not music."

"Rakim! Are you kidding me? He's a God. I got soul; that's why I came, to teach those who can't say my name. First of all, I'm the soloist," Urban sang again. "The soul controller. Tell her, Dad. Big Urban gets stronger as I get older."

"Can't roll with you on that one, son," Willie said, hunching his shoulders.

"Try some Luther Vandross," Maryland said. "Now that's what I call cool." And she broke into song.

Not only did she a look a lot like Teena Marie, the Caucasian songstress, she sounded pretty close to her, too.

"Ya'll sound horrible," Urban said, frowning.

"Unahh. They sound good," Jamillah disagreed, smiling.

"Shut up, you don't know nothing about nothing, ever," Urban said.

"Urban, stop that," Willie said with a firm voice that Urban knew meant business. "You don't talk to anyone like that, nevertheless your sister. Now apologize."

"Sorry, squirt," Urban said, reaching over and pulling Jamillah's pigtail.

"Stop it, you butt head," Jamillah cried.

"Both of you, cut the crap. You guys are messing up my Luther mood."

"Mine, too," Willie said.

"Now ya'll done put me in the mood for some Smokey. I don't care if they start to avoid me, I don't care what they do," Maryland started.

She looked at Willie for him to add his part, but his attention was on the rear view mirror.

Maryland turned around in her seat to see what had her husband's attention and what she saw caused her to jerk her body back around and stare straight ahead.

The siren went off and Willie pulled over on the right shoulder of the road.

"What in the world could this clown want? I know I'm not speeding," Willie said, checking the speedometer to make sure he was at or under the limit. He stopped the car and rolled down the window as the police officer approached.

"License, registration and a good 'splanation," the office said as he spat a glob of tobacco on the hood of the car.

Willie could see that this was going to be trouble. He turned around and looked at Urban. "This could get ugly. Do you remember everything I told you?"

"Hunh? I mean, yes, but why are you asking me that, Dad?" Urban asked nervously. He knew something bad was about to happen but he asked anyway. "What's wrong, Dad?"

"America," he said, turning his attention back to the officer and handing him the paperwork. "Now what kind of explanation are you looking for, officer?"

"'Splain to me why you riding around with a white woman at 'leven o'clock at night."

"Excuse me," Maryland said, leaning over her husband. "What kind of time warp have you been living in? This is my husband, you jerk. Give us our ticket and your badge number while you are at it."

"Shut yo' mouth, you nigga-lovin' bitch," he said and he reached for his pistol. "And you, get outta the cah, nigga," the officer said, pulling on the door.

Willie got out of the car, but not before reaching into the door panel and removing his .45-caliber handgun.

The officer reached to grab him but didn't know Willie was armed. Willie pulled away and placed the gun to the officer's head. The officer dropped his own gun to the ground.

The officer's eyes bulged out of his head and his bottom lip started trembling. He threw his hands up in surrender.

"You don't seem so bad now," Willie said calmly. "We have come so far in this country, but it's rednecks like you who refuse to move the hell on. So you think you can make it hard on people because you are so fucked up in the head. When you look at me, you should see a man and that's all. This is my family and I love them very much, and you don't even have to like it, but you must mind your damn business."

"Y…yes…sir," the officer stuttered as he nodded his head furiously. He closed his eyes and frowned as if he were trying not to cry. "Please don't kill me. I gotta wife and two youngins at home. Lord knows, they need me."

"My family needs me, too. Yet you are out here fucking with me. Why is that?"

"I made a mistake and I'm sorry," the officer cried. "Please."

"Are you really sorry or just sorry you didn't see this gun before I grabbed it?"

"I was wrong. And I swear to my Lord and Savior that if you let me go, I will walk away and let you good people go on about your business, if you spare me my life. Please."

"Why did you stop me?"

"I…I…I don't know," the officer stammered. "But I do know that I will walk away and let you be, if you spare me my life," the officer cried with real tears streaming down his face.

"I don't know. Men like you are not honorable. You are a racist. Your daddy probably was a racist, his daddy and his dumb-ass daddy. The world would certainly be better off without you."

The officer's knees buckled with fear.

"You have my tag number in your little computer and a man like you won't rest until this nigga"—Willie said, looking down at the man's pants and noticing a liquid stain getting larger by the second—"who made you pee on yourself, is dead. Am I right?"

"Noooo, sir," the officer said, shaking his head violently from side to side. "I swear on everything I deem holy that my word is as good as gold."

A pickup truck passed, paused, and then stopped. The brake lights illuminated, then went out as the truck pulled onto the side of the road.

"Is that you, Ned?" a voice sounded from the truck.

"Yeah, but you boys go on and get outta here. I'm alright."

The door to the pickup opened and a Caucasian male, who looked to be no older than twenty, walked toward them holding a shotgun. "Mister, you'd better put that gun down or this could get ugly."

"You better talk to 'em," Willie said, curling his lips into a snarl. "Who does he think he's going to hit with a shotgun from that far away? If he takes one more step, you *and* him are dead. And unlike you, my word is good."

"Cecil, stay where you are now, me and this man is just talking," Ned said.

"Then why he got a gun to ya?" Cecil said in a deep Southern drawl.

"Go home, Cecil!" Ned yelled.

"Can't do it," Cecil said, as he spat some tobacco onto the asphalt.

Maryland leaned over to the driver's seat and spoke out of the window. "Let's go, baby."

"I'm gonna get in my car and I don't ever want to see you again because if I do, I will not be so nice. Now back up."

Ned did as he was told but Cecil came charging forward with his shotgun. Willie turned the gun on Cecil and fired one shot, hitting him in the face. *Bam!*

Cecil was dead before he hit the ground. He turned the gun on Ned just as two more police cruisers pulled up. One was on the median with its headlights pointed at Willie, and the other had pulled up behind Willie's car. Both cruisers had blue lights flashing.

Ned, seeing that he had a little back-up, smiled and regained his confidence.

Willie knew this wasn't going to go well. If he surrendered, he was facing life in prison for killing Cecil. A black man killing a white man, even if it was self-defense, wouldn't sit too well in Georgia jury pools.

"Time's up, Nigga," Ned said, lowering his hands. "Now I know you think you a bad nigga but seem to me you are outnumbered and outgunned. Now get that gun out of my gotdamn face."

It was Willie's turn to smile.

Willie saw that the officer who had pulled up behind Ned hadn't gotten out of the car yet, but the one across the street had already taken up a firing position. There was a big rig coming up the highway toward them. Willie waited for the right time, then fired.

Bam!

He fired a bullet directly between Ned's eyes. Ned fell straight back and landed in the middle of the street just in time for a tractor-trailer to run him over. Before all eighteen wheels could finish passing over him, Willie was in his own car. He closed the door, turned the ignition, but before he could pull off, another police car pulled in front of him and opened fire, killing him instantly. Officers rushed the car with their guns drawn. Maryland had made the fatal mistake of trying to comfort her husband. One of the officers saw Willie's gun and opened fire on the helpless woman. She died five hours later at the hospital and, in the blink of an eye, Urban and Jamillah were orphans.

11

The telephone rang as Urban shook off the nostalgia of days gone by and gently placed his nephew in the nearby bassinet. He stood and walked over to the phone and checked the caller ID. It was the front gate.

"Mr. Brown, you have a visitor. She said she's your mom," the security guard said. "I have her name on the free entry list but she doesn't have any ID, so you'll have to verify her."

Urban grabbed his remote, flipped the television channel to the number two and saw Momma Winnie's face in the rear seat of a taxi.

"What happened to you guys the other day? My sister showed up with two guys and I didn't so much as get a phone call."

"I apologize about that, but the gate was inoperable for a few days and we were getting complaints that the residents couldn't get out, so we have to leave it open until we could get it fixed. It's working properly now."

"Send her in," he said, then hung up the phone and flipped the channel back to *SportsCenter*.

Two minutes later, he walked out of the door so that he could help Momma Winnie into the house.

"I can't stand stopping at that gate. Make me feel like I'm going to visit somebody in prison," Momma Winnie complained as she got out of the cab she was riding in.

"Oh, stop ya complaining," Urban said and reached into his pocket and gave the driver three twenty-dollar bills. He stopped midway when he saw who the driver was. A big smile creased his face. "Well, look what the cat done drug in. Raymond," Urban said, walking around to hug his foster brother. "I haven't seen you in ages."

"That's cause you don't come 'round enough."

"So you say," Urban said, stepping back to get a good glimpse of his big brother.

Raymond held out his hands for the payment. "Don't tell me you were about to pay a stranger and not hook your brother up."

Urban handed him the money. "Thank you, sir," Raymond said with a wide smile as he eased the money into his pocket.

"Shut up," Urban said before turning his attention to Momma Winnie. "Momma, you need to watch the company you keep."

"Hush that fuss."

Urban smiled and helped his mother into the house. Nothing made him happier than to have his family with him.

"I swear, every time I come over here, it makes me so proud of you. Who would've thought a trash man could live in a house like this?"

Urban shook his head.

"Yeah, man," Raymond said. "Whose trash you collecting, Donald Trump's?"

Technically, Urban was a scientist, but struck gold when his company found a way to turn household trash into renewable energy.

"So what brings you guys out here to hang with the common folks?" he asked once he got his mother settled.

"I came to get the baby."

Urban smiled and shook his head.

"His name is William and I already told you that I will not let you raise another child. He's fine right here with me."

"Boy," Momma Winnie said, "when do you have time to raise a child? You work fifty hours a week and when you ain't working, you up in the air somewhere headed to work. Now what kind of life do you think the baby gonna have if you ain't never home?"

"I'm moving some things around so I won't be gone so much and when I am gone, I'll bring him over there with you. How about that?"

Momma Winnie searched her foster son's face. "You really gonna keep him? Since when did you want kids?"

Urban hunched his shoulders and nodded to his nephew, who was sleeping peacefully in his bassinet.

"I'm hungry," Raymond said.

"What else is new?" Urban said as he tossed his head toward the kitchen. "Go ahead. Eat up."

Raymond was a big, hulking figure— six feet four inches tall, three hundred pounds, and if you looked at him from behind, all you would see was a big meaty head sitting directly on his shoulders. As a kid he was called, "No Neck." Gentle as a kitten with his loved ones and ruthless as a hyena with his enemies.

Raymond was one of the first people Urban had met when the lady from social services dropped him and Jamillah off at Momma Winnie's house. The other kids hadn't taken too kindly to the white boy with the half-breed sister, but Raymond and all of his girth put a quick end to that. "We all po' and don't nobody in here real momma and daddy give two shits about ya, so ain't nobody in here better than nobody else. White boy and his sister needs help just like we do, and I bet not catch wind of nobody fucking with 'em or it will be hell to pay. Test me out if you don't believe me. Test me out."

With that said, they were fast friends and, as time moved on, they became closer than any two blood brothers ever could be.

"What you got to eat, up in this sexy mutha?" Raymond paused to look around at the extravagant home. "Damn, this is a nice house, Urban. My little white brother is rich."

"Go eat, and watch your mouth, boy," Momma Winnie chastised as she sat down on the sofa. She rubbed her head as if the thirty-minute trip had sapped away all of her energy. "Can you grab me a cup of water, baby?"

"Yes, ma'am," Urban said as he walked into the kitchen with Raymond. Raymond opened the fridge, pulled out a one-pound pack of turkey, and took half of it. He peeled off four slices of American cheese, then grabbed the mayonnaise.

"I need some wheat bread," Raymond said with a straight face. "I'm trying to watch my weight. Doctor says I'm about sixty pounds over where I should be, but he don't know jack shit. I do feel like I can lose about ten, though."

"Oh yeah, if you lose ten pounds, you'll be beating the ladies off of you," Urban said sarcastically. "Diabetes and your hypertension will just go away."

"Shut up man. I got this under control, playa. Man, I've been putting in eighty-hour work weeks for the last three months. I ain't got time to be working out. I should've listened to Momma and got me a college degree or something. Driving that damn taxi all day hurts my ass cheeks."

Urban laughed.

"I'm telling you, man. It ain't no joke. Then you got women who call a cab, knowing they ain't got no damn money, then wanna try and offer you sex as a payment. High as gas is, I can jack off and get a nut. I need my damn money."

"Is that what you tell them?"

"Most of the time." Raymond smiled. "But sometime I tell 'em while they bent over the trunk of the cab taking it doggy style. Don't You, Try This No Damn More,"he said, gyrating his fat hips as he spoke.

Urban held his sides from laughter. He missed being around his brother.

"Well, make sure you try to take better care of yourself. We can't have you keeling over."

"Nah," Raymond said, stacking his sandwich. "You got some pickles?"

"Look in the door, man, lettuce, tomatoes. Everything you need."

"Damn, Sierra must've gone shopping. I know yo' ass ain't do it. I'mma put this mayonnaise back because it ain't good for my cholesterol level."

Urban chuckled as he looked at the mammoth sandwich. He grabbed a bottle of water for Momma Winnie from the refrigerator.

"You got some chips or something?"

Urban nodded to the bag sitting on the counter behind Raymond.

"Damn, if it was a snake, it would've bit me," Raymond said with his disarming smile.

When Urban walked back into the living room, Momma Winnie was asleep. He quietly set the water on the end table and tiptoed back into the kitchen.

"She fell asleep," Urban said.

"Poor woman," Raymond said. "She's one of God's angels. Always gives and refuses to take."

"So what's been going on with you, big man?" Urban asked.

"Same old thing, bro. But I'm hearing some bad things 'bout my lil' sis. Tell me it's just that folks done got too damn cold and now they exaggerating thangs just to have a better story to tell," Raymond said as he took a seat at the island and bit into his sandwich.

Urban sighed, pulled out a bar stool, and joined his brother. Just as he was about to say something, the baby started crying. He jumped up and ran to the living room to get his nephew before he woke up Momma Winnie.

"Look at cha," Raymond said as Urban walked back into the kitchen holding the child. "Daddy Dearest in this sexy mutha."

Urban cradled his nephew, checked his Pamper, and held him in his arms. He walked over and warmed a bottle.

"Being a daddy looks good on ya, boy," Raymond said. "It damn sho ain't for everybody. But it looks good on you."

"When are you going to have one?" Urban asked.

"Don't want any," Raymond said, dropping his sandwich. "I like being an uncle. Speaking of uncle, give me my nephew. He's too handsome to be in your presence. Some of that ugly might rub off on him."

Urban handed William to Raymond, walked over to the counter, and removed the bottle from the warmer. He handed it to Raymond and sat down at the island. He ran down the chain of events during the past weeks with his brother.

"Well, damn," Raymond said as he rocked the baby in his massive arms. "You been keeping him here every day since then?"

"Yeah," Urban said. "Thank God for lap tops."

"It's a good thing you're your own boss. Hell, I would've been fired by now. But I got something else to drop in your can, brother man. The police came by Momma's house looking for her."

"The police?"

"Yep, they said one of her friends ended up dead and they wanna talk to her. Now we all know Jamillah wouldn't hurt a fly, so she needs to get this straightened out and you need to get her a lawyer before she steps one toe in the police station cause you know how they question us...well, you don't know but when they question black folks, we normally don't make it out of there without some trumped-up charge being added on to what they saying we did."

Normally Urban would go off and defend his blackness, despite what his Caucasian skin said, but he was still in shock. His sister was wanted for questioning in a murder investigation; this was serious business.

"You know where she is?" Raymond asked.

"I have no idea." Now he was really scared for her. "She came by a few weeks ago wanting the baby. She said she was going to sell him."

"Sell him?" Raymond asked with raised brows. "What the hell is in that damn crack Jamillah smoking?"

"Yeah," Urban said, shaking his head in disbelief. He still found it hard to believe that his sister had sunk so low. "I gave her a few dollars and sent her on her way. Haven't seen or heard from her since."

"Looks like you need to call Priest," Raymond said just as little William burped and threw up on his shirt. "See," he said, handing the baby back to Urban. "That's why I invest in Trojans. Boy, you done messed up ya uncle's good shirt. I'll be doggon it."

Urban took his nephew and handed Raymond a paper towel.

"Priest," Urban said nodding his head. "I don't know why I didn't think of that a long time ago."

"'Cause you ain't smart as me. Nor half as pretty," Raymond said, flashing a gold tooth smile. "You need to holla at him like yesterday."

Priest Dupree was a police officer who had his own personal way of solving crimes. His way was wicked but effective. If you were on the right side of the law, he was your best friend, but if you veered left of what he considered right, you were as good as dead.

"Yeah," Urban said, nodding his head. "I guess I need to."

Momma Winnie walked into the kitchen. She stopped and stared at her two boys, then looked at the baby and smiled.

"Urban," she said. "I need to get on back home. Gather up the baby's things so we can get on the road."

"Momma," Urban said. "I already told you, he's staying with me. You've done enough."

"No," Momma Winnie said. "I've already found him a good home."

"He has a good home."

Momma Winnie stared at her son for what seemed like an eternity. "Are you sure?"

"Yes."

"Well, I see you already getting attached to him. Looking around at all this stuff you done bought him, he's already spoiled. Chile got more than some grown folks."

"What can I say?" Urban said, hunching his shoulders. "He's high maintenance."

"Okay," Momma Winnie said. "But if you need anything, you better call me and if he gets to be too much for you, call me. Like I said, I have a real good family who was looking forward to taking him in."

"You're number one on the speed dial," Urban said.

"Alright," Momma Winnie said as she gave Urban and the baby hugs. "Raymond, let's get on back to the house."

"Take care, baby bro," Raymond said as he headed out the front door.

12

Jamillah was getting out of the hospital. The four days she had spent being catered to and fed had done a number on her mind and body. She could run her fingers down the side of her chest and not feel the lumps from her ribs actually protruding through her skin. Even though she wanted to feel the sweet smell of crack cocaine entering her system, something inside of her was fighting that urge. Once the hospital had done all they could do, they told her she had two options. Go home or she could go along with the program and check herself into the rehabilitation place that Officer Vargas had suggested.

"Who's paying for this rehab?" she asked a skinny black nurse.

"Honey," the young nurse said. "If I was in your condition, I wouldn't ask any questions. You should've seen yourself when you came in here."

Jamillah didn't know what to think and she was too battered and bruised to argue. So after careful consideration, she decided that a few days in the hospital wasn't enough time away for those men to have forgotten about her, so she decided to continue take advantage of the state supported hideaway.

But the stay in the hospital had done something to her brain. Maybe it was all of those meds and fluid they kept pumping into her system. She was high out of her mind most of the time. Not the kind of high she was used to on the street, but high nonetheless. She was also a nervous wreck. The nurses were nice and worked around the clock to ensure that she found rest and relaxation, even if it had to be manufactured in the form of little white pills. The pills numbed the pain and helped her rest, but she had yet to relax.

Nightmares of those men killing Marcus were never too far from her thoughts. She could still hear him pleading for his life as the evil men laughed and toyed with him. But worst of all, she found herself jumping at the slightest little sound. A cabinet closing too hard, a door slamming shut, someone clapping his hands, everything reminded her of the gunshot that killed her friend.

What a horrible way to die, she thought. *And what a horrible way to live.*

That reflection she saw in the mirror alone was progress. Just a few short weeks ago, she recalled telling one of her smoking buddies that if she had to die, she wanted to die high. But not anymore. Not after what she had experienced with Marcus. She wasn't so sure how much she wanted to get high, but she was damn sure she didn't want to die. Over the last four days, her parents were heavily on her mind. It was as if they were staring down at her from the heavens above shaking their heads with disappointment.

Enough was enough. After she jumped out of the window and ran for her life, that redheaded, freckled-face man came running up on her with death in his eyes. She truly believed that he was the devil and she never wanted to see him again. She could still see him carrying Marcus over his shoulder, then tossing him into the dumpster like he was a piece of garbage.

Is that what I am? A piece of garbage, she wondered.

"What is your name?" Jamillah asked the skinny nurse.

"Veronica," the girl said with a smile.

"Girl, you need to eat," Jamillah said. "You ain't bigger than a fly."

"Ain't that the pot calling the kettle black," Veronica said rolling her neck. "I brought you some of my clothes to wear and you're sitting up here talking about me."

A look of confusion took over Jamillah's face. She looked down and did notice that she was wearing new clothes. "You mean to tell me," she said. "That you're bigger than me?"

"That's right," Veronica said. "Don't hate. Come on."

Jamillah got up from the bed thinking she didn't even remember getting dressed.

"So are you going home or to the center?"

"The center," Jamillah said.

"Good for you," Veronica said. "Take a seat. I have to wheel you out to the car that will take you over there. It's a nice place with real nice people."

"Good. I could use some nice people."

Jamillah and Veronica said their goodbyes. Jamillah got into a van that drove her about three or four miles away and down this long, winding driveway to a building that looked like a small college campus. They were met at the door by a woman named Amani.

"Jamillah," Amani said with a wide smile and opened arms. "Welcome."

Jamillah was a little skeptical of all of the nice people but she went along with the program and gave the lady a hug.

Amani showed her to her room and asked her if she needed anything.

"No," Jamillah said looking around at the room that was similar to her dorm room at Howard University.

"There are some books over on the shelf. I didn't know what you like so I put a little of everything in there. Even mine."

"So you're a writer?"

"I'm an aspiring writer; it's not published yet. The one I left for you is something I threw together at Kinko's, but I'm working on it."

Jamillah nodded, walked over to the books, and picked up the white paperback with a plain cover that simply said, *Thoughts.* She picked up the three street fiction novels with half naked women and gun toting thugs on the cover and handed them back to Amani. "I don't do these," she said.

"Good. Me either, but hey, I'm not a literary judge so I tossed these in with the rest of them."

Amani was a nurse, but to the residents, she was much more. She was around thirty years old, pretty as a baby, and very down to earth. Unlike most of the other nurses who were nice but never got too close to the patients, Amani wasn't afraid to show how much she cared. She was bold with her love. She never talked down to anyone, never led them to believe they were on the right track even if they weren't, and most importantly, she was firm. Every single patient loved her. To them, she was priceless, their very own Iyanla Vanzant. Amani loved talking about anything literary. She allowed the residents a first crack at critiquing her writings and even gave some of them a shout-out in the acknowledgment section of her novel, *Thoughts*. Some, if not most, of the therapy sessions turned into a regular book club meeting. That was until the supervisor showed up; then everyone quickly acted as if they were on the task of discussing their issues, but the minute the powers that be left, they were back at it. It was their own little secret. Little did they know, Amani's book was all about helping the helpless find themselves after years of being lost.

After about a week of keeping to herself, half attending the therapy sessions and overall being a recluse, Jamillah starting opening up. She and Amani became fast friends. Closer than most of the other residents. It was as if they were sisters from another mother.

"How are ya, girl?" Amani asked as she walked into the lunch room and sat down with Jamillah. "You're looking much better. Do you feel any better?"

"A little. I thought I stayed high on the street but, girl, ya'll got that good shit," Jamillah said with a wide smile.

"Oh Lord, what am I going to do with you?"

"Pray for me," Jamillah said. "Did you check up on what we talked about?"

"Still working on it," Amani lied. She wasn't allowed to do anything personal for the residents, but she realized, for many of them, she was all they had, so, on occasion, she would break the rules. But she wasn't about to get involved with what Jamillah was talking about. She opened Jamillah's chart. "You're gaining weight, girl," Amani said with a big smile. "You went from ninety-eight pounds to one-hundred-nine in your first week. Now you're up to one-hundred and fourteen. Blood pressure is moving in the right direction, too. I'm so proud of you."

"Oh, shucks, I'm getting fat. Let's celebrate with a drink."

"Sure," Amani said. "Sprite or iced tea?"

"You are such a hater."

"That's the truth because there is nothing that I could ever hate more than what my people allow drugs to do to them."

"Oh Lord, why did I get you started?"

"Because you know that's what you need to hear. But I'm not preaching today. I have things to do. Here..." Amani handed Jamillah about ten pages of her manuscript. "Don't be too hard on me now."

"I won't," Jamillah said, as she pushed her food aside and started reading. "Hey, wait a second."

"Yes," Amani said as she stopped and turned around.

"I'm still having those dreams. Have you read anything in the paper about anyone being arrested for killing Marcus?"

"No, I haven't."

"Was there even anything in there about him being dead?"

Amani shook her head again.

"So it's like he never existed."

Amani walked over and sat back down. She placed an arm around Jamillah. "He was a good friend to you, huh?"

"He was," she said as the tears began to fall. "He was a real nice guy. People didn't know it, but he was only twenty-one years old. Just a baby," she said, her words cracking. "Life dealt him a bad deck and he was dealing with it the best way he knew how."

Amani nodded and rubbed Jamillah's leg.

"I made an anonymous call to the police and told them I saw somebody dump a body in that dumpster behind that house I was staying in, so I know they know. They don't care about us. We're all throwaways to them."

"Who are the 'them' that you are speaking of?"

"Them," Jamillah said pointing at a white man who walked by. "The folks in control. The ones who make it hard on the have-nots."

"Is that what you believe, Jamillah?"

Jamillah gave Amani a look that said she didn't understand.

"It's not what I believe, it's what I know. They probably celebrate when one of us dies. Just a bunch of niggers killing other niggers; even if it was a white nigger that killed a black one. What do they call that? I can't think of it but it's when the wicked kill the wicked. Divine law or something like that."

Amani shook her head. "Listen, girlfriend," Amani said, "nobody owes you anything. In this world we live in, you must earn your own way. So the minute you decide that you are going to take your respect, I promise you, people will give it to you freely."

Jamillah dropped her head.

"You are not a nigger and neither was your friend, Marcus. Don't let his death be in vain. He died so you could live. And you won't let him down because you're special. You are somebody. You are a beautiful rose just waiting to blossom. You'll see. Right now, you're in the dirt but out of the dirt come some of this world's loveliest things. Now I can sit here and tell you that all day, but it won't matter until you believe it."

"There you go with your extra-positive ass trying to make me believe I'm somebody, when you know I'm just a crackhead looking for my next high."

"If that's what you believe you are, then that's what you are. If your days of using drugs are gone, then they are gone. Whether you believe you can or you believe you can't, you are absolutely right. Think about it. You are what you believe you are."

Jamillah nodded her head at the realness of what she had just heard.

"Are you done getting high or are you wasting everyone's time?" Amani asked.

Jamillah thought about the question. She was tired of lying, tired of hustling, and tired of being an addict.

"I'm done," she said, nodding her head. "I'm done."

"Good," Amani said as she stood. "Now let me get back to work."

"Bye," Jamillah said with a chuckle. "I got things to do myself."

PART
II

13

Lucinda Rawlings stared up at the ceiling with blurred vision. There was a pounding between her temples that made her head feel as if it might explode into a million little pieces.

The room was spinning and she couldn't figure out where she was. Lucinda tried to gather herself and make out what had happened to her. She sat up on her elbows and looked around the room. The living room's paneled walls were dark, and splattered with blood. But whose blood was it? She rolled over and heard the cracking of glass. It was her framed picture of Barack Obama and Joe Biden. She looked around the room and noticed that all of her pictures were scattered on the floor. Her home looked like a complete disaster area.

"What the..." she started, but her mouth hurt too much to speak.

Everything was in total disarray. The dresser was turned on its side, the bed flipped over, and all of the drawers' contents were emptied throughout the room. She looked around and realized that she was on the floor. Her clothes were torn as if she had been attacked by a chainsaw. Something was wrong with her eye. She felt it and it was swollen and she couldn't see anything out of it.

"What the hell..." she tried, but stopped again. She was in excruciating pain. Maybe her jaw was broken. She touched her mouth and felt the jagged flesh and immediately drew her hand back from the pain.

She tried to say something else but her mouth wasn't cooperating.

She rolled over onto her knees and pulled herself up to her feet.

Who in the hell would do this? But what had happened?

Lucinda staggered down the hallway of the single-wide mobile home.

She balanced herself on the walls as she made her way into the bathroom. She pulled the string to the swinging light in the middle of the water-stained ceiling and turned to the mirror. What she saw in the reflection almost scared the life out of her. Her coal-black face was covered with bruises and cuts. And that eye! Her left eye looked like something foreign plastered to her face. The reflection in the mirror looked like it belonged to an alien from another world.

She turned and ran as fast as she could down the hallway toward her daughter's room. She pushed open the door and looked around the tiny, immaculate room.

Empty.

"Keisha," she called, ignoring the pain from her mouth.

No answer.

Keisha's closet was open and Lucinda walked into the room and looked at an empty space.

"Keisha," she repeated and once again ignored the pain. "Keishaaaa!"

Lucinda hurried from the room, tripping over a pile of stuffed animals on the end of the bed. She found her balance and ran down the hallway and straight out of the front door.

"Help," she screamed, running down the orange clay dirt road toward the main road.

The people of Elkton, Georgia, came out onto their porches to see what all of the commotion was about. It wasn't unusual for screams to be heard in Elkton, but that kind of behavior was normally reserved for the weekends when the locals got drunk on moonshine and settled their issues with guns and knives. This was different; it was two o'clock in the afternoon. The residents who worked were at work, and most of the school-age kids who hadn't quit were at school.

"Help me, please!" Lucinda screamed, now oblivious to the pain from her lips and mouth as she ran throughout the trailer park. "Somebody help me!"

Maceo, the town's mechanic, walked out of his shop wiping his grease-stained hand on a dirty cloth.

Maceo was a character, but he was one of the most solid guys in the black community of Elkton. His word was good; his work was good; and if you were in his good graces, you were good, too. His appearance, well, that wasn't so good. He had a bald dome for a head, which was surrounded by gray hair on the sides, and he kept it in a processed curl. And to make him even sexier, he had a long ponytail. He had always been sweet on Lucinda, but her wicked ways kept him at a distance.

"Lucy," he called out. "Come here, gurl."

"That gurl is crazier than a bedbug," said Lawrence, Maceo's assistant.

"No, she ain't," Maceo replied. "Just a little misunderstood is all. Besides, who died and made you a psychologist?"

"Don't take no schoolin to know a fool when I see one," Lawrence spat back.

Lucinda turned toward Maceo and ran to him as if he were the last savior on earth.

"Good Lord," Maceo said, frowning as he took in the sight of the battered and bruised woman before him. "What happened to you?"

"Somebody attacked me!" she screamed through large and deep breaths.

"Somebody like who?" Maceo asked. He reached into his pocket for the two-shooter Derringer pistol he kept there.

Lucinda shook her head. "I don't know."

"You don't know? Well, what kind of company you keeping, Lucy? You been drinking again?"

"No," Lucinda said, holding the side of her face. "Get me over to see Dr. Smith. I can't breathe too good and my mouth feels like it's broke."

Maceo hesitated a second, then nodded toward Lawrence. "Get my truck, man."

Lawrence looked at Lucinda and shook his head. "Probably tried to beat somebody outta they money and got what she had coming," he said, taking his time.

"Didn't ask for yo' opinion, Lawrence," Maceo chastised. "Now get my truck."

Under normal circumstances, Lucinda would've used her sharp tongue to tear Lawrence a new rear end, but she didn't have the energy to go there today.

"Lucinda, gurl, you gonna have to watch the company you keep," Maceo advised as they waited on the truck.

"Somebody broke in."

"And took what?" Lawrence asked over his shoulder. "Some rotgut liquor? Lord knows, that's all you got up in that raggedy-ass trailer."

"That's bout enough outta you, Lawrence," Maceo said. "And I ain't asking you no more to get that truck. If you got a problem with that, then keep on walking. You can find you a new job."

Lawrence grunted at Lucinda, then slowly walked into the shop to retrieve the truck.

"Lucy, what would somebody break in yo' house fo'?" Maceo asked.

Lucinda looked at Maceo for what seemed like forever before answering. "Keisha."

"Keisha? What do you mean, they took Keisha?" Maceo said as his face frown into a snarl.

"She gone," Lucinda said as she fought back the tears.

"Lucy," Maceo said, rubbing his gray beard. "Keisha's eighteen years old now and she's been running around here telling anybody who wanted to hear it that she was moving to Lanna."

"But why?" Lucinda couldn't stop the tears from flowing. "Why she gone up and leave me? Ain't I been good to her?"

"Sho you been good to her, but she's young and full of ideas," Maceo said. "Lord knows, ain't nuttin' 'round henh for a young gurl with a good head on her shoulders."

"Moved to Atlanta with who?" Lucinda asked. Her mouth was killing her, but she loved her daughter too much for any kind of pain to interfere.

"I don't know. Maybe with Harris. You know they running round here talking about getting married since they already acting like husband and wife. Being that they got the baby and all."

"I'll kill his li'l ass if he takes my baby."

"It wasn't Harris that broke in was it?" Maceo asked.

"No," Lucinda shook her head. "This was a big man."

Lawrence pulled the truck up and Maceo walked around and opened the passenger door to the old Fred Sanford-like beater. He helped Lucinda in and closed the door once she was buckled up.

He walked around and jumped behind the wheel. "Lawrence, watch the shop for me."

Lawrence nodded at Maceo and gave Lucinda a nasty look.

Maceo and Lucinda rode in silence the two and a half miles it took to get to the small clinic that stood as the town's hospital.

Elkton, Georgia, was a small town where eighty percent of the population operated below the poverty level. And it was very much a town divided by race. The Blacks lived on the east side of the tracks and the Whites lived on the west. The only thing that was integrated was the trailer park. Even there, the Whites felt they were better because the majority of them had double-wide trailers and most of the Blacks could only afford single-wides.

Maceo parked in the emergency spot in the clinic's parking lot and helped Lucinda out of the truck. He walked her through the front door of the single-story, red-brick building and called out to a nurse for help.

An elderly white woman wearing a white jacket and a stethoscope rushed over. "Lucinda, honey, what happened to you?"

"Somebody attacked me," she moaned.

"Who would do such a thing?" Dr. Smith asked. She was a small white woman who seemed to be genuinely caring.

"I don't know, Dr. Smith," Lucinda said, shaking her head.

"You don't know?" Dr. Smith examined bruises as she led Lucinda into a room off of the main hallway. "Have you been drinking?"

"No," Lucinda snapped, already frustrated with the questioning. "And nobody else bet ask me that no damn mo'."

"Okay, okay. I'm sorry," Dr. Smith said, trying to calm her down. "Have you called the police?"

"I ain't got no phone."

"I'm going to have to call them and report that you were assaulted."

Lucinda jerked her neck toward the door. There was a tall man walking out of the building. He was wearing a white coat with fur around the hood.

"Who is that man?"

Dr. Smith turned around just before the man walked out. "Don't rightfully know who he is. I didn't treat him."

"That's him," Lucinda said, trying to get to her feet to follow the man. "That's the fool who attacked me."

14

The morning's dew was beginning to fall. The street lights were still on and the people of the night were starting to head in to make way for the working folks.

Urban drove through a dilapidated neighborhood near downtown Atlanta known as "Vine City." Crackhead hookers walked up and down Simpson Road, hoping to catch a quick "date" before daylight arrived and took away their natural cover. Teenage drug dealers tossed their heads up in a nod, hoping to find a matching sign from the people behind the wheels of the cars. Urban watched as car after car pulled over, made the quick drug transaction and went on about their way. Urban sighed and kept his eyes straight ahead. He was trying to find a particular street. He looked in the rearview mirror and noticed an unmarked police cruiser had started tailing him.

A stray dog with patches of her hair missing and sagging teats took her time crossing the street, practically begging Urban to run her over and take her out of her misery. When Urban slowed down to allow her to pass, she showed her teeth, giving him the canine version of the middle finger.

The cruiser's blue lights came on and Urban pulled over. He turned on his car's interior lights and reached for his license and registration. Every time a police got behind him, he couldn't help but think about his parents and the tragedy that followed.

"Urban Brown, you ugly son of a bitch," Agent Priest Dupree said.

"You must not have any mirrors in your house, Priest," Urban said with a smile as he stepped out of the car and gave his old friend a hug.

Priest Dupree was an imposing figure. Standing six feet four inches tall and weighing about two hundred and forty pounds, he wasn't to be taken lightly. He was a man of the people and a complete terror to those who crossed him. Two years ago, when police officers in Atlanta were robbing drug dealers, Priest singlehandedly put a stop to it. He killed one of the officers and beat the other one so badly that he resigned from the force and started working at a Wal-Mart. The move didn't make him very popular in the police department's locker rooms, but that's how he was—always standing for what he felt was right. Priest was also a legend. He went undercover as a drug dealer for three years, infiltrating and bringing down the largest drug cartel in the United States. His personal life was a little sketchy. Only a select few knew that he had a wife and a daughter. He went to great lengths to keep his family out of harm's way. Urban happened to be one of those select few who knew the real Priest.

"Since when did you start driving police cars? Did you get a demotion?"

"Nah, man. I'm working on a little pet project and gas is too damn high to be using my own car."

"I see you're still cheap."

"Not cheap, baby boy. Smart. I'm sorry I wasn't able to get back with you right away. I was on vacation."

"No problem, man. Thanks for recommending Ms. Patty. I would've never thought of her."

"*Her*." Priest smiled and shook his head. "It's amazing what time will do."

"Yeah." Urban smiled in return as he thought about the peculiar man/woman who had served as the neighborhood's daycare provider.

"How's Momma Winnie doing these days?" Priest asked.

"She's fine. Still fussing and trying to save the world."

"Good. Well, tell her I asked about her."

"Will do."

"I know you couldn't go into too much detail on the phone, but what's going on with ya?"

"Jamillah," Urban said, shaking his head. "That girl is trying her best to get herself killed."

"What's going on? Talk to me."

"Lots of drama, man. To make a long story short, Jamillah is on the run. I hear some white guys beat her up because she reneged on a deal she had with them to sell my nephew," Urban said, nodding to the back seat where his nephew was sleeping peacefully.

Priest stuck his head in the truck and took a glimpse of the little guy. "Good-looking fella. Ms. Patty will keep the goons off of him."

"I hope so. Jamillah brought those goons to my house, and I don't know if I'm being paranoid or not, but I could've sworn I've seen those guys creeping through my neighborhood."

Priest nodded.

"Then I hear that the police want to question her about a murder," Urban said, sighing away his frustrations. "This is crazy."

Priest kept his poker face. "Murder? Jamillah! That girl couldn't kill a roach."

"You know that, I know that, but I'm not sure if the police know that."

Priest turned and walked to his car. "Do you remember how to get to Ms. Patty's house?"

"I think so."

"Turn right at the light and Ms. Patty is at the end of the street on the left. Old raggedy-ass green house. You can't miss it. I'll meet you over there in a minute. I need to check the system and see what I can find."

"Sounds good. See you in a bit."

15

Ms. Patty was actually Mr. Patrick. He/she never hid her sexuality. Standing at a miniature five-feet–one inches tall and maybe one hundred pounds soaking wet, she was hell on wheels. She commanded the respect of the neighborhood either with a kind word or a quick draw of her gun—which was almost the same size as she was.

"I swear fo Gawd, I'll bust every cap I got in this bitch," she would say, aiming her gun at whoever wronged her and she had done a few years behind bars for doing just that.

Ms. Patty was almost seventy years old and had been living as a woman so long, most people didn't have a clue what her true gender was. Every morning, she rose from her bed and put on her makeup, dress, and stockings as if she were a real woman.

Urban knew that Priest trusted Ms. Patty with his life. So when he recommended the transvestite matriarch to watch his nephew, he didn't hesitate. He was very familiar with her strict guidelines on who she would allow in and around her space. He also knew that if anyone came around snooping with ill intentions, they would get far more than they had bargained for.

"Hey, child," Ms. Patty said as Urban pulled up in front of the rundown green house.

Urban jumped and looked around. He didn't see anyone but the voice was unmistakably that of Ms. Patty.

"I'm back here," she said, walking from the side of the house. "Had to empty out some fish grease befo' those chillin' start showing up. Got my house all stank up. I love me some good croaker, but that doggone smell makes me sick to my stomach."

"Aren't you looking lovely?" Urban said with a wide smile. He walked over and hugged her.

"Tell me yo' name again," Ms. Patty said, looking up as she recognized him but couldn't place a name with the face. "Those sho is some mighty fine threads you's wearing, fella."

"Urban Brown," he said. "Momma Winnie's boy."

"Hush yo' mouth," Ms. Patty said, slapping Urban's arm. "I don't know how I forgot you. Must be getting old. You was the only little white face running round here and yo' lil' ass was bad, too," she said with a smile.

Urban smiled and shook his head. "I see you're still taking good care of yourself. You look good," he lied. She actually looked a hot mess—an old man with caked on facial makeup, gray arched eyebrows, bright red lipstick and a sun dress in the winter time.

"Oh, hush yo' mouth, boy. I don't look no different than I always looked. Don't shoot me no shit, chile. But you looking good." Ms. Patty looked him up and down and openly flirted. "Fine as some red wine fresh off the grape vine, unh."

Urban frowned inside, but kept a straight face. "I need a favor," he said, anxious to move on to the next subject.

"As long as said favor ends with some dead presidents," Ms. Patty said, rubbing her fingers together, "we can talk. I stopped doing' *favors* long time ago. Folks take advantage of you and my temper too hot to be getting taken advantage of. I spent three years on the chain gang for busting a cap in a fool after I did a damn favor that didn't end up with them dead presidents in my possession."

Urban pulled out a few hundred dollars bills and handed them to her. "This is my nephew and I need a 'safe' place for him to stay during the day, while I'm at work. I should have everything straight in a week or so. I'll give you two hundred a week, if that's okay."

"Two hundred dollars a week is fine, but you ain't gotta pay me that much. One hundred will do and you ain't gotta worry 'bout nobody messing with him. That you can count on," Ms. Patty said as she placed the money in her bra. "I'll take this other hundred as a deposit."

Urban smiled.

"Don't mean to get in yo' business, but what's wrong with Winnie's place?"

"Wanna keep her out of this for a minute…"

"Say no more." Ms. Patty waved him off. She walked around, pulled on the back door handle and opened the door. "Come here, lil' fella. What's his name?"

"William," Urban said, loving the way his nephew's name sounded.

"Gotcha. Be henh to pick him up no later than six-thirty. I can get expensive if you keep me away from my bingo. Is everything in this baby bag?"

"Yes, ma'am. I should be here around five. If I'm late, I'll call and make sure I have those presidents."

"Who is that, Priest?" Ms. Patty asked, looking at the unmarked car that pulled up.

"Yes. We have a few things to discuss."

"Oh Lord," Ms. Patty said, shaking her head as she walked toward her house with little William in her arms. "Whenever somebody brings me a child and Priest shows up outta nowhere, that can only mean one thing."

"What's that, Ms. Patty?"

"Shit 'bout to hit the fan," she said as she made her way up the steps to her porch. "But whatever is crooked, he gone get it straight. You can best believe that."

Urban walked over and sat in the passenger seat of Priest's car. He gave him the entire rundown from the time he got the call from Momma Winnie up until the very moment they were sitting there. Priest nodded and took mental notes. He flipped his lap top computer screen around so that Urban could see the image of Jamillah's haggard face.

"She's in the system and she is wanted for questioning. I'm going to hit the streets and shake some trees. In the meantime, you go on with your daily routine. I'll holla at you when I know something."

The sight of his sister made him miss her. He hated what drugs had done to her. But every time he said he was through with her, visions of his mother and her last words echoed in his head. *Take care of your sister.*

Priest got out of the car and walked around to the passenger side where Urban was getting out as well. They did the brotherly hug. "I'll get to the bottom of this, Urb. Don't worry yourself to death. Don't you let the white boy come out of you and start jumping outta windows," he said. "Ya'll will kill yourselves over the smallest shit."

"I'll try to stay on the ground." Urban smiled. Hearing the taunts about his race made him think of the good old days where a single hour didn't go by without him hearing how stupid or scared white people were. The funny thing about that was he never considered himself any different than any of the other faces he was around. Life was a struggle for all of them.

"How's that pretty girlfriend of yours?" Priest asked.

Urban shook his head and closed his eyes.

"Damn, boy, you already ran her off?"

"I hope not."

"A good woman is hard to find, bro. So if you have a good one, you might as well figure out a way to deal with her bullshit and get you some sleep," Priest said as he balled up his fist and touched Urban's. "I gotta go. I'll holla at cha soon."

"Take care, man, and thanks for your help on this."

"Not a problem. You do the same. I'll holla at cha when I get something."

Urban got into his truck and slipped on his seat belt. As he put the vehicle in reverse, he looked at the empty car seat and missed his nephew already. It was amazing to him how he could fall in love so fast. He was indeed head over heels for his nephew and made a vow to himself that he would die before he allowed anything to happen to him. It had been almost three weeks since he'd picked him up and this was the first time he was out of his sight. How would he get through his day?

16

The lights on the top of Jethro Watson's Ford Explorer lit up the evening and the siren roared as he briefly paused and sped through every traffic light he encountered. He wasn't in pursuit of *anyone* but rather *something*. He hit his brakes as he passed the dirt road that would be a shortcut to his destination. He placed the truck in reverse, slammed it back in drive and sped down the orange clay dirt road. His tires skidded and slid, but they found traction and he was off to the races.

Jethro's entire life was centered around being a police officer. He was single with no kids. His only responsibility outside of the police department was a Boxer puppy named Sam. Jethro was actually smarter than people gave him credit for. He was the sheriff of Elkton County and he had won the election by a landslide. However, that had more to do with the behind-the-scenes signal callers who were tired of the incumbent rather than anything Jethro had done. Most people thought Jethro was an incompetent ingrate whose daddy had paid for the election before he died; it was more true than false.

Jethro's physical appearance didn't do anything to help his appeal with the locals. He was tall and skinny, with a huge head and had a doofy Gomer Pyle manner. And when he wasn't parked behind the grocery store, stealing a nap, he was at the jail sitting at his desk reading the *Atlanta Journal Constitution* online. Jethro had big dreams of solving big-time crimes, but nothing major ever happened in Elkton. The most he would run across was a petty theft or a driving under the influence charge. Occasionally, he would get an aggravated assault charge when the locals had too much to drink and got to carrying on with brass knuckles. Sometimes it would be an occasional knife fight between guys who would be friends again once they calmed down. Now, he had a real bona fide crime on his hands—a breaking and entering, a real aggravated assault, and the granddaddy of them all—a missing person.

Jethro couldn't contain his excitement as he smiled ear to ear thinking about the hunt that lay ahead. Finally, he would show these country bumpkins what he was made of. He pulled in the parking lot of the town's clinic and parked in a spot reserved for emergency vehicles. After all, this was an emergency. He jumped from his truck so fast that he left it running. When the car started rolling backward, he jumped into it, his feet skidding and sliding as he tried to gain control of the vehicle. "Damn it," he said as he finally got it in park and removed the keys.

One of the orderlies laughed as he watched Jethro fight with the vehicle. Once he was out of the truck, he slipped on a patch of ice and fell flat on his butt. "Damn it," he said again as he turned on his knees and got to his feet. "I want someone out here right now to put some sand or salt on that ice. The whole damn county will be broke if someone falls and breaks a limb."

The orderly continued laughing, but didn't budge to retrieve the salt or dirt.

Jethro gave him a hard look, pointed at him, but fanned him off. He had bigger fish to fry and a big-time crime to solve. He walked down the corridor to the nurses' station and got the info he was looking for.

"Get yo' ass away from me, Jethro," Lucinda yelled through her wired jaw.

"Now, Lucinda, I gotta investigate this thing so we can find who did this to you. I'm here to help you and you gotta cooperate."

"You couldn't find a hooker in a ho house with ten twenty dollar bills. Now get yo' ass outta my face," Lucinda spat. She had no real reason to hate Jethro. It was just that he represented everything and everyone she blamed for her shortcomings. In other words, he was White.

Jethro's eyes bulged. He couldn't believe what this ungrateful fat heifer was saying to him. In his eyes, he was the law and didn't take kindly to her insults.

"I have a good mind to arrest you right now for hindering an official police investigation, but I'm going to let you slide 'cause you…"

"I wish you would try to put some damn handcuffs on me. I will beat yo' ass like you stole something. Now get outta here. I ain't telling yo' dumb ass nothing. Go on 'bout yo' business, Jethro. I ain't playing wit you."

Jethro had had enough. He closed his notepad and snarled at Lucinda.

"Well, Ms. Rawlings, you have it your way," Jethro said, removing his handcuffs. He grabbed Lucinda's arm, but she snatched it back and smacked him so hard his hat flew off. She did all of this while lying on her back.

"Put yo' damn hands on me again and I'ma knock the stank off of ya," Lucinda growled as she tried to sit up.

Jethro took a deep breath, got his footing, and dived on top of Lucinda. She caught him and squeezed him so tightly that he screamed, "Okay, okay, okay!"

Jethro stood and caught his breath; he backed up and knocked over the monitoring station and a bunch of other medical devices.

"Doggone it, Lucinda, you going to jail," Jethro said as he caught his breath. "Now I don't want to shoot you, but I will. You're already going down for resisting arrest. I can add assaulting a police office to the list, but I'm not, 'cause you sick and that just won't sound right."

Jethro pulled out his gun. That only enraged her more. "You gonna pull a gun on me?" she said, ignoring her pain, and getting up from the bed. She stalked toward Jethro as he retreated.

Even with the gun, Jethro was afraid. He backed up out of the room and called for help. A few nurses came running.

"I'm about to shoot her," Jethro said as he continued to back up into the hallway. "Somebody better get this woman."

"Jethro, put that gun away," Dr. Smith said as she walked up on the chaotic situation. "What's gotten into you?"

"That," he said, pointing at Lucinda as he huffed to catch his breath. "She's going to jail for resisting arrest and interfering with an official investigation and I'm going to think of a few other charges to add on for being disrespectful."

"Oh be quiet, Jethro," Dr. Smith said as she led Lucinda back into her room.

"I don't have to be quiet. I'm the law and I'm trying to do my job," Jethro said.

"Slow your roll, cowboy. I'll bring her down there to talk to you once she's healed up," Maceo said as he walked down the hallway.

Jethro, seeing that he was outnumbered and wasn't going to get any help with this beast of a woman, placed his gun back in its holster. "I want her in front of me no later than six o'clock tomorrow evening. And I mean it. If not, I'm coming back and I'm going to arrest everybody who is in this hallway. Y'all gonna start showing some respect to the law."

Jethro turned on his heels, stomped back into the room, retrieved his hat, and stomped out of the hospital.

Everyone in the hall started laughing and shaking their heads at the very entertaining state of Elkton's law enforcement.

17

It was three o'clock in the morning and the entire facility was quiet, but Jamillah couldn't sleep. She was trying to read, but that didn't help her either. She couldn't get her mind off of Marcus. His death affected her more than anything she had encountered in her life as a drug addict.

Jamillah stood, walked over to the freestanding wall locker where her clothes and personal items were kept, and quietly got dressed. She crept to the door and peeped into the corridors. They were empty, so she eased out of her room and made her way down the deserted hallway and through the back door. Once outside, she walked across the dewy grass and into a different building which was right behind the one where her room was located. She had been off the streets for three weeks and she was experiencing a little hint of cabin fever.

Jamillah used her identification badge to pick the lock on the door. Once inside, she flicked on the light switch. The low-watt bulb over the sink came on and that was enough illumination for what she had in mind. She sat on the floor, straightened out her legs and began to stretch. She touched her forehead to her thigh for twenty seconds as her hamstrings screamed in pain. She leaned down, placed her head between her legs and gave her quads the same attention. She stood and turned the treadmill on to its lowest setting and began a warm-up walk. Slowly she increased the speed until she was where she wanted to be. The leather belt of the treadmill was turning fast and Jamillah was struggling to keep up. Her heart rate increased until it felt as if it were going to jump out of her chest, but she wasn't about to quit. She needed a victory and she would take this small one. She hadn't worked out in years, but in recent weeks it seemed that running was all she had done. The only sound that could be heard was Jamillah's heavy breathing and her sneakers hitting the leather belt of the treadmill.

The light came on and she jumped, almost falling off of the machine.

"Hey!" A man's voice shattered her peaceful predawn workout. "What in the hell are you doing in here?"

Jamillah removed the safety key from the display board and the tread-mill went off.

"What are you doing in here?!" the man barked.

Once she was composed, she got pissed. "I'm working out," Jamillah snapped. "What does it look like I'm doing?"

"Breaking the rules," the security guard said in a gruff tone. "Now you could be in big trouble for being in here."

Jamillah sighed and shook her head. She walked over to the scale and stepped on.

"Hey! Did you hear me?"

Jamillah ignored the man and checked her weight. She smiled to herself as she realized she was making progress. She had gained a few more pounds. To a lot of people, a few pounds meant nothing, but to her it was a ton and it meant that she was slowly but surely getting back to her normal self.

"What's your name?" the guard asked. "Where is your ID card?"

"I'm not in jail, man. This is a voluntary thing. Do you know the meaning of *voluntary*? Now move your fat ass out of my way," Jamillah said, trying to walk around the heavyset guard.

"It might be voluntary, but you still need to follow the rules. I need your name. I'm writing you up."

"Well, you'll have to make something up because I'm not telling you a thing."

The guard frowned. Jamillah could tell he wasn't used to being spoken to in this manner.

"Oh, so you're one of those smarty pants, uppity-ass bitches, huh?"

"Will you move out of my way, or do I need to scream for someone to come here?"

That comment made him step back. He looked into her eyes and searched to see if she was the type to make good on her threat. He nodded his head and backed up with his hands up in a truce.

"Okay, listen," the guard said. "Maybe we got off on the wrong foot. I'm Officer Tucker. I apologize for scaring you. I'm new here, so let me make it up to you."

"No thanks. Just let me go back to my room, since you already ruined my workout."

"Why don't you work out during the day like everyone else?"

"Because I like my quiet time and being that it's no longer *quiet*, I'd like to go back to my room, if you don't mind."

"You're a feisty one, ain't cha? Okay, but I'm still going to insist you let me make it up to you." Officer Tucker pulled out a little plastic bag.

Jamillah's heart rate increased more than it did when she was on the treadmill. The mere sight of the oh-so-familiar white rock caused a great deal of conflict within her. She stood there staring at the little bag. She couldn't move.

How could this thing have such a hold on me? she wondered.

It was like showing a starving man a plate of filet mignon, a baked potato, and a side of broccoli with cheese. Before she knew it, she had reached for the bag, but Officer Tucker pulled it back.

"What do you what?" Jamillah asked, fully expecting him to unzip his pants.

"Nothing. I want you to forgive me," the guard said with a wicked smile.

Jamillah's eyes bore into the man. She knew there was more to it than that, but if that's all he wanted to hear for a slice of heaven in a pipe, then so be it.

"Forgiven," she said, snatching the bag from his hand.

"Now," he said. "There's plenty more where that came from."

"And what in the world could I have done for you to be so generous?"

"Nothing as of yet, but I'm sure the day will come when you can help me out."

Jamillah nodded her head knowingly. She grunted at the sorry looking man before her, then walked out of the room.

18

Jethro sat at his desk surfing the department's Internet database. His puppy, Sam, was at his feet chewing on an old shoe and trying to get Jethro to play with her. Jethro wasn't in the mood to play doggy games. He was hard at work searching for crimes similar to the breaking and entering and subsequent kidnapping at Lucinda Rawlings's place. He wasn't having any luck and he was getting restless. His instinct told him there was something big about this case, but he couldn't put his finger on it. However, he knew he was going to get to the bottom of it.

Jethro logged off the computer and stood.

"Sam, let's go get into something. We can't solve any crimes sitting around here like a bump on a log."

Jethro grabbed his hat and picked up Sam and they headed out to his police cruiser. He took the liberty of driving over to where the Blacks and poor white folks lived. He had to check out Lucinda's place. Any police officer worth his salt had to check out the crime scene. He pulled up in front of the trailer, and waved at two black kids who looked to be about ten-years-old. The boys were playing baseball with a tennis ball and a broom stick. Jethro pulled Sam out of the car and the kids dropped their sticks and ran over to him.

"Can we play with her?"

"Sure," Jethro said, He loved kids and held out hope that he would one day have his own. "Not too rough; she's only two months old."

Jethro left the kids and Sam, walked up the raggedy steps, and turned the doorknob. It was locked. He walked to the back and tried that door. He was tempted to pull out his gun and shoot the handle off, but that would make too much noise; and in this neighborhood, it might get him shot.

He walked back to the front and approached the bigger of the two boys.

"Hey, big guy," Jethro said. "I need a favor."

"Sir."

"How old are ya, son?"

"Nine."

"Big boy. Why aren't you boys in school?"

"Teacher work day."

"Oh. Vacation time, huh?"

"I guess."

"Do you mind getting in that window for me?"

"I can't do that. Mrs. Lucinda will whip my tail."

"I'm here trying to help her. Someone broke into her house and beat her up. I'm her friend and I'm trying to put the person in jail who did this."

The little boy nodded. "Okay," he said, "lift me up."

Jethro lifted the kid up to the window and like an expert, the little boy fiddled with the window's lock and crawled through. Fifteen seconds later, he walked out of the front door.

"Thanks, little buddy," Jethro said, handing him two dollars.

"Thanks," the boys said in unison and went back to playing with Sam.

Once he walked inside, he did a double-take at the total ruin before him. The place was a mess, but somehow he could tell that the lady kept a clean house. And, no surprise to him, she had definitely put up a fight. The blood stains on the wall bothered him and he wished he had a forensics person on staff who could take samples and help solve this crime. He walked into the kitchen, which was clean as the board of health, and searched the cabinets for a plastic bag. Nothing. He went to his car, got a first-aid kit and used the cotton swabs and plastic bags to collect and carry his evidence. He also found a broken watch that belonged to a male and the granddaddy of them all, a pistol. He smiled to himself for getting such a big lead and headed out of the trailer, locking the door behind him.

"Okay, big fella's. We need to get going. Come on, Sam," Jethro said to the boys. He called out to Sam and she looked at him as if she really didn't want to leave. With a little whistle from her master, the puppy took off toward Jethro. "You boys be good."

"Yessir. Bye, Sam," they said, before running back to their makeshift baseball game.

Once Jethro got back to his office, he pulled up the type of handgun he had collected. It was a Glock 36, shot a .45 round, and cost about six hundred dollars.

Lucinda Rawlings was a drunk with a loud mouth. It wouldn't be too farfetched for someone to have gotten tired of her and taken a beating to her. But that didn't seem like the case.

Where was the daughter? Was she there at the time of the beating? Did the daughter do this? Did she have something to do with it? Did they have a disagreement? There were so many questions running rampant in his head.

Jethro looked at the clock. It was already eight o'clock and he had told Maceo to have Lucinda at his office no later than six. Just as he prepared to leave to go and arrest Lucinda, Maceo walked in.

"I was about to come looking for you," Jethro said.

"Whatchu looking for me for?" Maceo asked.

"Well, you took responsibility for bringing in Ms. Rawlings. And as you can see, she ain't here."

"Dr. Smith won't release her. She got a broken jaw and a whole lot mo' is wrong with her."

"Do you have any idea who would do this to her?"

"Can't say that I do, but she said she seen the boy at the clinic who did this. One of the nurses gave me this to give to you." Maceo handed Jethro a paper with a name on it.

"Thanks. Is this the fella Ms. Rawlings said assaulted her?" Jethro asked excitedly. He couldn't contain his joy at getting another big lead.

"Yep, that be him. I need to get back to the shop."

"Wait a second. Where did she get this name?"

"Said the boy came in there looking to put something on his bleeding hand and arm. I guess Lucy bit him pretty good. She's a firecracker, that's for sure."

Jethro nodded like he was edging Maceo to tell him more, but no luck.

"I see. I have a quick question for you, Maceo," Jethro said. "Where could I find Ms. Rawlings' daughter?"

"Lucy say she missin'. Said she don't know where she is, but personally,

I think she took the baby and went to Lanna. Just my opinion; ain't got nothing scientific to back it up with, but that's my gut feeling."

Jethro grunted. "What gives you that feeling?"

"Elkton ain't no place for a youngun' like that. She full of ideas and ain't much of them ideas gone get her 'round here."

"You said she had a baby. You know the baby's father?"

Maceo nodded his head.

"Care to share his name with me?"

Maceo thought for a few. He didn't want to give up his own nephew to the white man. It was comforting to know that his nephew was a good young man. Never had an ounce of trouble in his entire life. "Dominique, Dominique Thomas."

"Address?"

"I've told you enough."

"Thanks, Maceo," Jethro said. "If I need you, can I call on you?"

"Yep. I'll tell you what I know, which ain't much."

"I appreciate what you've done. I'mma try to help get this guy who did this to Ms. Rawlings. Even if she thinks I can't find him, I'll get him."

Maceo hunched his shoulders as if he didn't have much confidence that Jethro could deliver on his promise.

"You don't believe me, do you?"

"Ain't 'bout what I believe. If you feel like you can hunt him down, then hunt on. Any man who would do this to a woman, don't deserve to walk 'round free. And he ain't no man in my book, but hey…" Maceo shrugged his shoulders. "So I hope you do catch him."

"I'm gone do it, you watch," Jethro said, nodding his big head. "I'm 'bout to run this name through the system and see what I find. You wanna hang around?"

"Nah, I got business to tend to. So I'll let you tend to yours. But keep me posted," Maceo said.

"I thank you for bringing me this and if you don't mind," Jethro said, easing closer and leaning down to Maceo's ear, "keep this name between us. Wouldn't want any information leaking out that might hinder the investigation."

"I hear ya, Matlock. Do what you do; don't worry 'bout me spilling the beans," Maceo said before walking out. "You take care."

"I'ma still need to interview Mrs. Rawlings. Will you tell her that?"

"Yep," Maceo said as he walked out of the front door of the small building.

19

Urban couldn't remember the last time he had been this happy. Having little William around had opened up a joy in his heart that he never knew existed. But still, there was something missing, and when his phone rang, he knew exactly what that something was.

"How've you been?" Sierra said.

"Hey," Urban said with a big smile. He also could tell by her tone that she wasn't calling for drama purposes and that she was willing to bury the hatchet. "I'm well. What about you?"

"I'm fine."

"Well, I couldn't be better."

"Is that right?"

"Yeah." Urban sighed. "Well, I kinda miss this certain hotheaded woman."

"Hotheaded?" Sierra asked. "Have you been seeing someone else that quick? And why in the world would you miss her if she's so hotheaded?"

"Because she's kind of cute and her sex is something to behold."

"Aww, man, you can find a cute girl with some good sex anywhere."

"See, that's where all women go wrong. I can find sex anywhere, but good sex…well, that's a different story."

"Whatever—if it has breasts, men will jump on it."

"Wrong," Urban disagreed. "I dropped William off this morning at the daycare with a transvestite and she had on a bra, so I'm assuming she had breasts, but I would rather die a slow and painful death before I would ever touch that thing. However, I'm going to let you and all of your close-minded sisters keep thinking that."

Sierra laughed.

"I've had about twenty or thirty replacements since my girl left, and none of them could match her."

"Are you are trying to get your Brady Quinn-looking head knocked clean off?" Sierra asked.

"Nope."

"Well, you better clean up your act, buddy."

"When can I see you?" Urban asked.

"After you tell me how the baby is doing."

"He is stealing my heart by the second. You better hurry home before he steals it all."

"Aww, I don't mind losing your heart to him. I wanna see him. What has he been doing?"

"What does an infant do all day? Smile, boo boo and burp. He's trying to crawl. Looks more like he's humping the floor, though."

"Oh my God," Sierra said. "Do you have that child over there watching pornographic movies?"

"He might've gotten into my stash. I need to go check that out."

"You are out of control. I spoke with Raquel and she said he was really healthy and that he was going to be a heartbreaker."

"The boy has good genes. What did you expect?"

"She also said you are trying to spoil him. Please tell me why you are putting him in those high-priced clothes when he doesn't know a Polo from a chitterling? What in the world does he care about Jordan's?"

"Well, he has to be fly," Urban said as if his nephew wearing high-end clothes was a given.

"Oh Lord. When are you free to see me?"

"Well, I just got into my office, but I can leave. I *am* the boss."

"I can be at your place in an hour. I'm leaving the airport."

"Okay," Urban said, not even bothering to turn on his computer. "I'll see you then."

"You know we still need to get some closure on this Jamillah thing, don't you?"

"And here I was in a good mood."

"We don't have to talk about it now, but we need to get it settled."

"Sounds like a plan."

"Bye, baby."

Baby! That could only mean one thing. Sierra was in the mood for a little more than forgiveness.

Urban was tempted to head over to Ms. Patty's place to pick up little William but he needed to see his girl. Both of them could use some much needed alone time.

20

Urban pulled up into his circular driveway and slowed down. There was a light on inside of his house that he knew he didn't leave on. Or maybe he did. No. He never left that light on. He could sense immediately that something was out of whack. Instead of hitting the garage door opener, he pulled close to the house and stopped. Still looking up to the second level where the light was on, he thought he saw a silhouette. Either his mind was playing some serious tricks on him or someone was in his house.

Urban kept his eye on the top floor as he reached into his glove compartment and removed his handgun. He eased out of the truck, being careful not to slam the door. He walked around to the rear of his house and searched the perimeter. He walked up the steps of his deck and peered into the windows of the French doors that led into his house.

"Whatchu doing over there, Urban?" Vincent, Urban's elderly next-door neighbor, said as he stood on his own deck watching his dog mosey over to Urban's yard and take a dump. "I'll pick that up a little later."

Urban looked at him but didn't respond. There were at least fifty yards between Urban's house and Vincent's place so the old man had to yell pretty loud for Urban to hear him. Urban didn't want to alert anyone to his presence; he placed his key into the lock and turned the knob slowly. The door chime from the alarm didn't sound and that confirmed all of his suspicions. He chambered a round into the barrel of his weapon. He eased the door open, expecting to see his place ransacked, but everything was pretty much undisturbed. Nothing was thrown about but someone was his house; this much he knew. He dialed the authorities on his cell phone.

"Nine-one-one, what's your emergency?" a male's voice asked.

"I'd like to report a breaking and entering in progress," Urban whispered. "I'm not sure if they are still on the premises, but I think they are."

"Address, please."

Urban gave the operator the address and the man pried for more information, but Urban ended the conversation.

I just told that fool a person was in my house. Obviously this is not the time to be chit chatting, brainiac.

Urban stood in the living room and waited. His back was against the wall and his pistol was aimed straight out in front of him, locked on the staircase. He heard footsteps in William's room directly above him.

Urban tried to control his breathing. He had to remain calm, yet his heart rate increased by one hundred percent as he felt his nerves shifting into overdrive. He was tempted to unload through the ceiling and exterminate whoever was brazen enough to break into his house, but he resisted the urge.

He heard the footsteps make their way toward the staircase and hurry down them. He aimed the gun right at the bottom of the steps. The minute he saw the man's face, he fired.

Bam!

The man screamed like a schoolgirl, ducked, and ran for the front door.

Bam!

The man fiddled with the locks and shot out of the door before Urban could give chase. He wasn't sure if someone else was with him and was coming down the stairs firing their own weapon at him, so he was careful not to get too excited. He eased around the sofa and out the front door just in time to see the police car coming up his street. He ran out to the street and flagged down the officer.

"I shot at this guy; he was in my house. He was wearing jeans and a big black coat. There he is," Urban said, pointing at the man who was coming out of a neighbor's yard. Just as Urban pointed, the man darted back between two other houses.

The officer nodded and sped off to give chase. Urban made a beeline to his neighbor's house. Vincent was being nosy as usual and met Urban halfway across his yard. He was carrying his shotgun.

"Vincent, did you see anyone in my yard?"

"Yeah," Vincent said, making a big exaggeration of cocking his gun for Urban's sake. "You need some help?"

"Not sure. Tell me what you saw?" Urban asked in a rushed tone.

"There was a car sitting out front of your place for a few minutes. I was out getting the paper for Martha. You know she don't like to walk early in the morning because she had surgery on her hip about a week ago and the doctor told her…"

"Vincent," Urban said, waving him down before he went off on a ten-minute tangent. "The car. Tell me about the car."

"Oh yeah," Vincent said. "A black guy got out and I think it was a white guy driving; not sure, but I think so. The one who got out, walked up to your front porch and rang the doorbell, and then a few seconds later, he went in. Hell, I thought it was one of your buddies," Vincent said. "I know you have lots of black friends, so hell, I just thought it was one of your friends."

"What kind of car was it?"

"I don't know for sure but it looked like one of them souped-up numbers. You know the ones them Mexicans drive. I know it was blue. And it was white. And it had big old tires on it."

Urban remembered seeing a car that fit that description when he pulled onto his street. The car was driving away from him. Maybe when they saw him, they pulled off. He didn't think anything of it at the time.

"Did you see anything else that looked out of the ordinary?" he asked Vincent.

"Oh hell, Urban, I don't know, man. I tend to mind my own business. Like I said, being that you have lots of black friends, I didn't think nothing of it."

"Okay, thanks, man," Urban said.

"What's going on?"

"Don't know. Somebody broke into my house."

"Shit, Urban, we pay good money to live here and I don't take too kindly to those kinds of people coming around here disrupting our peace of mind. This is a gated community. How in the hell did they get in the goddamn gate?"

"I don't know, Vincent," Urban said, walking back to his yard.

"I'm damn sure going to find out," Vincent said, storming back across his yard.

Urban stood in his driveway, confused. The man he took a shot at was dirty, with a raggedy beard and soiled clothing. Everything about him said, drug addict. Could this be Jamillah coming back at him for taking the baby? She did seem rather desperate. Urban pulled out his cell phone and called Priest.

"What's cracking?" Priest answered.

"I shot at some guy who broke into my house."

"What?"

"Yeah. A policeman came and he's looking for him now. I saw him running down the street. I'm not sure if this is random or if it's connected to Jamillah."

"A'ight," Priest said. "I'll be over there in about thirty minutes. Tell the officer to stay put until I get there."

"Okay." Urban tried to figure out what in the world was going on.

Suddenly, the police officer's car raced back toward Urban's house and stopped in front of him. The officer jumped out and motioned for Urban to come over. There was a man in the back seat.

"Is this the man you saw?"

"Yeah," Urban said, staring hard at the man who was just an uninvited guest in his house. Something about the man was really familiar. "That's him."

21

Priest pulled up right before Sierra's taxi dropped her off.

Urban changed directions and walked over to his woman. He was so happy to see her that even after what he had just encountered, he couldn't stop smiling. He gave her a soft kiss on her even softer lips. He embraced her for a long and firm hug. Holding her made him feel like the world was a beautiful place even with all of the chaos surrounding him.

"Did you miss me?" Sierra said with her own smile.

"More than you know," he said, savoring the sight of the beautiful woman standing before him.

"What's going on?" She nodded at the car and the tall man sitting on the hood of what appeared to be an unmarked police car.

"Baby, take the keys to my truck and drive to your place. I'll explain everything later."

"Hunh?" Sierra asked with a worried expression as she reluctantly took the keys from Urban. "What are the police doing here?"

"Somebody broke in."

"What? Are you serious? Were you in the house?" she asked with grave concern.

"No, I wasn't here."

"Oh, my God!" Sierra almost screamed. "Are you sure you're okay?"

"I'm fine. I came home and saw a light on. So I called the police. When I went inside I saw the man and he ran off. That's pretty much it, but we'll talk about it later."

"Is that him in the back of that police car?"

"Yeah, I think he's one of Jamillah's friends, but I'm not sure. He's not in a talking mood," Urban said, pointing at the rough-looking man who was now handcuffed and being escorted out of the car toward Priest.

"What in the world is going on?" Sierra said.

"Baby, I will tell you as soon as I know something. I don't want you to go in the house until I can make sure that it's safe. So until then, go to your place."

"Yeah, yeah," Sierra said, nodding her head. "I'm sorry to keep you."

Urban could tell she was apprehensive, but given that the dust hadn't really settled on their last argument, she decided to go along with it. "Call me the minute you know something."

Urban kissed her again and walked her over to his truck, placing her luggage in the back seat. After she was safely buckled in and backing out of the driveway, he walked back to Priest, who had the perpetrator penned up.

"Who else was with you?" Priest asked the man.

"I ain't saying shit," the man said. "Get me a lawyer."

Priest told the uniformed officer that he would take responsibility for the suspect. The officer balked a little, but Priest motioned him over and led him off where they could have a few words in private. Ninety seconds later, the officer was smiling and shaking Priest's hand. Then he walked over to the suspect to remove his handcuffs.

"Will you go inside and check the place out and let me know when it's clear?" Priest asked the officer.

"Sure thing," the officer said, all of a sudden willing to cooperate with anything Priest asked of him.

The burglar rubbed his wrists where the handcuffs had been. "I don't know why you assholes always put the cuffs on so damn tight," he complained, looking around as if he was thinking about making a run for it.

"I wish you would," Priest said, reading the man's thoughts. "I will shoot you down like the rabid dog you are. Now move your ugly ass."

Priest pushed the man toward Urban's house. "We'll use the garage so we can get these neighbors back to whatever they were doing before they started looking out of their windows."

Urban felt a sense of embarrassment as he looked around and saw one of his neighbors peeking out of parted windows. He knew he would be answering questions for the next two weeks about all of the commotion and police activity at his house.

"So you're going to take the fall for this all by your lonesome, potna?" Priest asked as he shoved the man down onto a stool that was used for a work bench.

"Ain't shit to me," the man said in a cocky tone. "This lil' breaking and entering ain't 'bout jack, man. I won't get thirty days for this shit. Judge gonna throw this out. Plus that cracker damn near shot me. I should file charges against his ass."

"Oh yeah, that should work out for ya," Priest said.

"Old white broad sued McDonald's for hot coffee and got paid. I bet you I could get a few g's."

"What are you going to do with a few g's in jail, dickhead?"

"Ya momma's a dickhead," the guy said. "Besides, jails too damn crowded to be fooling 'round with a petty-ass burglary. And as far as I'm concerned, that's all it is."

That last statement confirmed for Priest that the man's presence in Urban's home was indeed far more than a break-in. But what could it have been? The man's ratty appearance and overpowering stench said that he was a man of the streets and more than likely a substance abuser. Didn't seem that he would venture this far out without a car to commit a burglary.

"You're right," Priest said. "You're a pretty smart dude. Did you go to law school?"

"Yeah," the man said, displaying a plaque-caked smile. "The school of hard knocks."

"And I'm sure you graduated magna cum laude."

"What?" the man asked with a frown. "Look here. Lock me up or turn me loose. I ain't got time to be sitting up here with y'all fools. Fo' I know it, y'all be done tryin' to pin something on me. I ain't got nuttin' else to say to you clowns."

"What's your name?" Priest asked.

"George Bush."

Priest chuckled. "You are a real funny man. So how long have you been smoking crack?"

"How long ya momma been selling it," the man replied. "Take me to jail or let me go. I ain't got time to be up here with yo' renta cop-looking ass."

"What else do you have to do?" Priest asked calmly.

"Don't you worry about what the hell I gotta do," the man said, rising to his feet. "Now either send me to jail or let me get the hell on 'bout my business. You stalling 'cause you know you ain't got shit on me. Hell, I'll tell the judge I thought this was my girlfriend's house and when I realized it wasn't, I left. I was leaving when this cracker started shooting at me. I should whip yo' ass, cracker. You could've shot me, gotdamn it," the man said, faking a punch at Urban who didn't bother to flinch.

"Is your name Allen?" Urban asked as he finally remembered where he knew the man from. Ironically, the man standing in his garage was the same man who had tried to rob him the night he went to rescue his nephew.

The man shot Urban a look. "Who in the hell is you?"

"Not important," Urban said. Now he knew there was something to this, but he was going to let Priest do what he was good at. "But let's just say this makes you zero for two with me."

"What?"

"Hey, sit your simple ass down," Priest said. "I have a question for you; it's rhetorical, but answer if you like. Whoever said anything about you seeing a judge?"

The man smiled, but it was obvious to every one in the garage that he didn't find anything amusing. He looked around as if he were checking for an escape route.

"My name is Priest," he continued, handing him a business card. "Priest Dupree."

The man read the card and his smug smile faded into a fearful gasp. It was obvious that the name had conjured up something within him that wasn't very pleasant. The arrogance and confidence he'd shown moments ago was now a distant memory.

"Now sit your raggedy ass down," Priest ordered.

The arresting officer walked back out of Urban's home and gave Priest the thumbs-up. "All clear," he said. "I even checked the attic."

"Good job," Priest said, nodding at the officer. "I'll give your supervisor a call and tell him what a good job you did."

"Thanks." The officer smiled.

"Hey, man, take me to jail. Please, man," the perpetrator pleaded with the officer. "That fool is crazy."

"You're in good hands," the officer said before walking down the driveway and getting into his car. He pulled off and the suspect stared out of the window at the fleeing police officer as if he was his last hope.

Priest watched the officer and waited until he was moving down the street. Then he turned to face the suspect and fired a punch to the man's face, knocking him out of his chair.

Urban grimaced at what had to be a bone breaker to the man's bony face.

"You will talk and you can start with your name."

"Man, what the fuck…" the man started but was punched again.

"Nigga…" he said, trying to get up from his knees.

"I asked you your name," Priest said.

"I ain't no punk," the man spat.

A punch, then a kick to the ribs, and another punch found their marks.

"I have all day," Priest said, pulling the man back to his feet.

He punched the man again, knocking him down to the garage floor where he moaned in pain and held up a hand to stop the continuous assault. "Wait, man, shit!" the man screamed, holding his bloodied lip, bruised eye, and mangled cheek. "I'll tell you what I know. Damn, I ain't signed up for all this shit. Not for no funky-ass two hundred dollars."

"What's your name?"

"My name ain't important. I'ma give you the number to the white boy who paid me."

Priest reached over and took a crow bar from a tool rack hanging over the work bench. "I will not keep hurting my hand fucking around with you."

"Come on, man," the guy begged.

"You will give me what I ask for or I will try my best to bend this steel bar around your nappy-ass head. Now you can start with your name!" Priest barked.

Urban had some reservations about Priest's methods. All he could think of was someone doing the same thing to his sister, yet he forced himself not to interfere.

"Allen Paulson," the man said, shielding himself with his forearm. "And I got a few warrants for some…so just go ahead and lock me up, man, please."

"Shut up," Priest said with a grin. "Now, if you work with me, I can make those warrants disappear. This doesn't have to be that hard or painful."

"Man, you're playing games. I don't know what the hell kind of cop you is."

"A very good one. At least that's what I like to think. Now," Priest said, extending his hand, "it's nice to meet you, Mr. Paulson."

"Whatever!" Allen grimaced in pain and refused the hand.

"Tell me, what were you doing in this house?"

"This white boy paid me two hundred dollars to come in here and get a baby."

Urban's heart sank. His antennae shot straight up once his nephew was mentioned. A threat to little William was a threat to him. And now he wanted to take Priest's place and beat the man into oblivion, but he remained calm. He walked over to Allen. "Where is Jamillah?"

"Who?" Allen asked with a face that said he was either a hell of an actor or he didn't have a clue.

Priest raised the crowbar. "Keep playing that stupid role and I promise you, you'll be unconscious in less than two minutes."

"I don't know no Jami Allah, man, or whatever you said his name was," Allen said, ducking behind his arm. "All I know is this redheaded white boy picked me up, gave me a hundred dollars, and told me he would give me the other half when I brought him the baby. That's all I know. I swear to God."

"Shut up," Priest said. "You think your swearing to God means anything?"

"I don't play with God now. Damn all that," Allen said with pursed lips. "I might be a lot of things but I ain't crazy. God's off limits, gotdamn it. I grew up in the church. I don't play that shit."

Priest shook his head. "You know in all of my days of dealing with you fools, you have to be the craziest of them all."

"Wait a minute." Allen reached for his pocket. "I got the redhead's number right here. He told me to call him when I got the baby."

"How do you know this guy?"

"I told you. He was riding through the 'hood. I thought he was looking for something good to smoke on, ya know? I was gonna try to hustle his ass, but I'll be damned if he ain't hustle me. Got me up in here dealing with Priest Dupree," Allen said, shaking his head. "Man, you a dirty-ass cop. Folks in the 'hood can't stand yo' ass."

"Shut up," Priest ordered. He had heard it all before. Actually, hard-working people loved him; it was the thugs and lowlifes who hated the air he breathed. "So you make it a habit of jumping in cars and agreeing to kidnappings?"

"Hey, man, listen," Allen said, getting somber. "I'm on them narcotics kind of bad. I ain't saying I'm proud of it or due no special treatment because of it, but the man offered me two bills. Do you have any kind of clue how fucked up I can get with two hundred bucks? Nigga, I'll be high for a week and a half. 'Cause I be buyin' that good shi…"

"Hey." Priest snapped his fingers. "Stay focused. Finish your lie on the redhead."

"Whatever, man, I told you I don't lie. You know what? I'ma fight yo' ass when I get in shape," Allen said, frowning at Priest. "I ain't no damn punk, man."

"The story, Allen," Urban said.

"Oh, yeah. He said the baby belonged to his sister and the baby's daddy was trippin'. So, hey, I was just tryna make a few bucks. I wasn't tryna hear all that Judge Mathis family drama shit. 'Cause like I said, I gets higher than the stars in the sky. Ya'll square asses should loosen up and try a hit of that crack. Whooodiewhooo. I'm telling you, it ain't nuttin to play with."

Priest looked at Urban, who was searching Priest's trained eye for signs of lies. Priest nodded that he believed the guy was telling the truth.

"Call him," Priest said.

"Call who?"

"The guy who asked you to bring your simple ass up in this man's house."

"I swear to God, one of these days, I'ma put a foot in your ass, Priest," Allen said. "You can mark my words on that one."

"Yeah, I'll be waiting. Make the call, Allen."

"Hey," Allen said, looking at Urban with some recognition. "You the same white boy I damn near killed a few weeks back, ain't ya?"

"Yeah," Urban said. "Thanks for sparing my life. Now make the call."

22

Jamillah was staring at the crack cocaine like it was a long-lost relative. It had been about a month since her system had felt the exhilarating effects of the potent drug. She was conflicted. She had worked really hard to cleanse herself, but here she was willing to throw all of that hard work out of the window just to go back to where she was. A tear fell from her eye as she vacillated between throwing the drug away and smoking it. She smiled to herself because last month at this time, she wouldn't have even considered throwing a lint-size piece of crack away, nonetheless a nice twenty-dollar piece like she was staring at now.

She could actually taste it; she could feel it entering her system and delivering that oh so satisfying high. Her breathing increased as she made her mind up. She would smoke this one and be done. *One for the road*, she told herself. She jumped up and decided it was time to go, time to leave the facility. She had gotten everything she needed. She felt that she had learned enough on how to resist the urges and temptations that she would encounter in the streets.

Jamillah sat back down on the bed and laughed at herself. *Who am I fooling? And why am I even trying?* She jumped up again, walked over to the closet, and tossed all of her meager belongings into a backpack. She had made her choice. She was an addict and maybe that's all she would ever be. She needed to feel that crack in her system and nothing was going to stop her. She finished packing, closed her closet, and looked out of the window. The world was a cold place and maybe she wasn't strong enough to handle it. Maybe she was meant to be an addict. Either way, she had to smoke this crack. At least this one last time. There was a light tap on the door that snapped her out of her thoughts.

"Good morning," Amani said, walking in. "Are you going somewhere?"

"Umm," Jamillah stuttered. "I was about to go for a little jog. You know, work out some stress."

Amani looked at the open locker and saw that it was empty. She looked down at the bag by Jamillah's feet and frowned.

"Do you need to take all of your things to work out?" Amani asked.

Jamillah was busted and she could read the disappointment on Amani's face. She slumped her shoulders, signaling that she was defeated. "You know, this place has been great and you have been even better, but I'm not ready. I appreciate you more than you'll ever know, but like you guys always say, nobody can help you if you don't want to help yourself. I'm not sure I'm ready to help myself right now."

Amani sighed and nodded her head. "Will you at least pray with me before you leave?"

Jamillah thought about the request. She knew in her heart that God wanted nothing to do with her. Especially now that she was turning her back on all of the grace He had shown her. But right now, the devil was winning and he was telling her to go on and say a fake prayer in order to get back to the wonderful feeling that he could provide her. That crack was burning her pocket and begging to be inhaled into her lungs; she would pacify the do-gooder.

"Sure," she said.

Amani walked over to her and sat on the bed. She patted a spot next to her and Jamillah sat down. Amani held out her hand and Jamillah laced fingers with her.

"Before we pray, I have one question for you."

"Okay," Jamillah agreed, losing her patience. She wanted to get high and Amani was wasting precious time.

"If not now, when?"

"I'm not sure I understand that question."

"You've shared with me a lot about your family. Your mother, your father, and your brother. Based on what you told me, your parents were people of great honor. So if you're not going to start being the person they gave their lives for right now, then when will you?"

Something about what Amani said, hit her like a ton of bricks. The tears returned.

"I don't believe in God."

"Yes, you do. That's merely a lie you started telling yourself when you decided to sing in the devil's choir. But you are a believer, and more important, He believes in you. You are never too dirty to come home. You are never too soiled to be forgiven. He is God, not some person on the streets who might pass judgment. He will forgive you; all you have to do is ask."

"If He believes in me so much, then why don't He ever help me out?"

"Are you kidding me?" Amani said. "People pay up to ten-thousand dollars a month to be treated at this place. Tell me, how much are you paying?"

Jamillah thought about it, but didn't have an answer.

"Your friend was killed, but you weren't even shot. Sure you had a few bumps and bruises, but look at you now…you are beautiful. And yet you sit here with crack in your pocket taking advantage of all of what God is doing for you."

Jamillah's expression turned from guilt to shock to anger. Had she been set up?

"What are you talking about?" Jamillah said as she jumped up and assumed a defensive posture.

"Come here." Amani stood and walked over to the window. "You see that?"

There was a police car out front. "We have cameras in every corner of this place. We are serious about the business of getting people back to where God intended for them to be. And we don't tolerate our own employees working against what we are trying to accomplish. That man who gave you that crap is sitting in the back seat of that car. Those same police are out there waiting on you to step one toe off of these premises with that drug in your possession so that they can slap the handcuffs on you. Now you've come too far in your journey to throw it all away because you faced a challenge. Rise up and beat this. Now the choice is yours."

Jamillah's mouth fell open. Faced with those consequences, what choice did she really have?

"You're better than this," Amani said, holding out her hand. "And God willing, if you make a commitment to yourself, the next time you're challenged like this, it won't even faze you."

Jamillah was speechless. She reached into her pocket and removed the crack. She handed the little plastic bag to Amani. Amani reached out and gave her a hug. Jamillah welcomed the embrace as she struggle to free the demons that had lived inside of her for far too long.

"I wish I could flush this crap down the toilet, but the police said they need it as evidence."

"Yeah." Jamillah nodded. "I'm sorry for letting you down."

"It's not about me. You're a human being and as humans, we are far from perfect. We all fall, but the test comes when its time to get up. You've had these drugs in your possessions for hours. Yet there are still here. That's a victory right there."

Jamillah thought about what she had just heard and nodded. Yes, she was getting there, but there was still too large of a piece of her that wanted to get high.

23

Lucinda felt as if every bone in her body was broken. She gingerly lifted herself up enough to press the little red button that released the pain-killer. She didn't feel anything. She had pressed it so many times, that maybe there wasn't any more left. She pushed another button to call the nurses. A few minutes passed, but no one came. She had harassed them so much that now they ignored her.

"Hey!" she yelled. "I know y'all hear me! If I get up outta this bed, it's gone be some problems. And why the hell ain't nobody get in touch with my daughter?"

Lucinda had been asking about Keisha ever since she arrived. She had her ways, but she always took great pride that she gave her all for her only child. And although every cell in her body screamed in pain, nothing ached as much as her heart. She had been in the hospital for three days and every second was spent worrying about Keisha.

Keisha was all Lucinda had. Her mother and her father had died a long time ago and her sisters and brothers chalked her up as a drunk. They hadn't said three words to her in the last ten years. Even during the holidays, they would call and speak to Keisha but never to her. Sometimes her siblings sent Keisha birthday or Christmas cards and at times, they would even add a few dollars in there but there was never as much as a sentence inquiring about Lucinda. Without Keisha, did she really have a reason to live?

And Caleb! Oh how she missed her grandson.

Why would Keisha just up and take everything away from me? she wondered. But even as the thought formed in her head, she already knew the answer. And she couldn't really say she blamed the girl for leaving; she would've done the same thing if the shoe was on the other foot.

What kind of mother would leave a brand-new baby with someone who couldn't stop drinking? Even if that someone was his own grandmother. Depression had set in a long time ago and now that she was all battered and bruised, she didn't know which way to turn.

Lucinda tried to sit up, but the pain of her broken ribs felt like she was being stabbed with the jagged end of a pitchfork. It forced her to lie back down. The sight of Jethro standing in the doorway only dropped her spirits further.

Jethro walked into the room and eased over to the bed. He didn't want to upset the injured woman, but he needed answers so that he could move his investigation along and finally get to the bottom of this mess.

"Now, Mrs. Rawlings, I think we got off on the wrong foot. I'm not the enemy. I don't know what I've done to you, but whatever it is, I apologize. I'm only here to help you."

Lucinda was too beaten to fight. She closed her eyes and nodded her head.

"Should I call a nurse in here? You don't look so well," Jethro said, genuinely concerned about the woman who had never said a kind word to him.

Lucinda nodded. She was in too much pain to fight.

Jethro turned and walked to the door. He used all the authority his voice could muster when he yelled out for a nurse.

"What kind of place are you people running here? This woman in here needs some attention. She's lying here writhing in pain and ya'll ignoring her. Don't you have some kind of epidural or something ya'll can give her?"

A nurse came walking down the hallway toward the room. "She's at her limit already, but I will give her a little more."

"Thank you kindly," Jethro said, touching his forehead and nodding as if he were tipping his cap. "I mean I thought people came to the hospital to make them feel better not put them in more pain."

Lucinda smiled with her eyes, showing her appreciation to the lawman as the drugs made their way through her system. She welcomed temporary reprieve from the pain and closed her eyes before dozing off to a sound sleep.

Jethro sat with Lucinda and watched her stir in her unconscious state. It was as if the she were fighting with someone in her dreams.

Poor woman! She can't even find peace in her sleep, he thought.

When Lucinda opened her eyes, Jethro was sitting in the chair in the corner, reading the *Atlanta Journal Constitution*.

"Jethro, you still here?"

"Yes, ma'am," he said, jumping to his feet. "You need anything?"

"Some water."

Jethro walked over to the counter and poured a glass of water from the pitcher.

"Thank you."

"No problem."

Lucinda swallowed the water and took a deep breath. "I'm sorry I treated you mean. You're a nice man and didn't deserve that."

"No problem. You been through a lot."

"Still no cause to act like that."

"I don't mind. Truth be told, I'm kind of use to folks treating me that way," he answered. "Can't say I understand it, but…"

"Well, I appreciate you getting those dumb nurses in here to help me out."

"You're welcome. Mrs. Rawlings," Jethro said apprehensively, "tell me what happened."

Lucinda shook her head at the memory. "Me and my grandbaby was taking a nap. When I woke up, this man was standing over me with a gun in my face. I tried to grab it and he hit me. I hit him and we 'bout tore the place up. He got the best of me 'cause I was drinking, but if I was sober, he wouldn't had a chance. He hit me with something hard. Coward of a man, you know. Couldn't fight me with his hands. Had to get something to hit me with. Anyway, I seen Keisha and I tried to call her, but that hit I took made me a little woozy. Before long, all I see is darkness. I guess he knocked me out."

"You said your daughter was there at the time?"

"I can't say what time she got in, but for some strange reason, I see her at the door. Almost like she scared of the man. I think. I can't be sure on that 'cause like I said, I was drinking. But I know I saw her at the door. Don't know if she was coming in or leaving out."

"Have you ever seen your attacker before?"

"No," Lucinda said, shaking her head. "But I'm sure that was him I seen leaving here."

"I'm checking that out."

"You been by my house?"

"Yes," Jethro said.

"You seen, Keisha?"

"No. I can't say that I have."

"She hates me. She told me she was leaving me and that she never wanted to see me again."

"Well, I wouldn't put too much stock in that. She probably just wants you to stop drinking. It's the alcohol she hates. Not you."

"So you Dr. Phil?"

"No, ma'am. Just a thought."

"Go on with your questions."

"Do you think that Keisha may have had anything to do with you being attacked?"

Lucinda rose up on the bed and glared at Jethro. Her once calm face curled into a snarl as if she was about to show her fangs. All of a sudden, she snapped, "What the hell kind of question is that? That's my only chile. You 'bout a dumb sonafabitch to even think something like that. Black people don't hit they elders like you white folks. Simpleminded-ass, cracker. Now why don't you take yo' old retarded-looking ass right up outta here fo' I jump up from this bed and put sumpin' on you that you won't ever forget."

Jethro stood and shook his head. He was lucky to be able to receive what little information he got. He looked down at Lucinda.

"I'm only trying to help. I'm not the enemy."

"Well, enemy yo' ass out that door."

"I hope you get better soon, Mrs. Rawlings."

"Yeah," Lucinda said. "And I hope you learn how to stop asking dumb ass questions."

And with that, he turned on his heels and headed out of the room. Even with the lack of cooperation, he was determined to solve this case.

24

"What I'm s'pose to say?" Allen asked Priest, who was standing over him with a cell phone in his hand.

"Say what you would say if you were successful with your little boneheaded scheme," Priest said.

"Man," Allen said. "Why you gotta be getting smart all the time. How come you can't just talk to a nigga like he somebody."

"Shut up."

"What's in it for me?" Allen asked with a straight face.

"I'll tell you what," Priest said. "Not that I owe you anything, but I believe you're telling the truth so after you do this, not only will I cut you loose with no new charges, but I'll get rid of those old charges that are hanging over your head. I might even give you a few bucks."

"How I know you ain't lying? I know cops take a class in lying," Allen said.

"Shut up. You're not in a position to ask questions. Besides, you might be the one that's lying."

"Man, I ain't lied since nineteen seventy-six," Allen said, smiling and already counting his take in his head. He closed his eyes and inhaled, leaving no doubt about his plans for his cash.

"This is a knock-off phone; you can't trace it, so I want you to call Mr. Redhead and tell him you have the baby."

Allen shrugged his shoulders and reached for the phone. He dialed the number.

"Yo, man, I got the baby," Allen said "Whatchu want me to do with him?"

There was silence on the other end of the phone.

"Hello," Allen said.

"Yes."

"Whatchu want me to do with the baby, man?"

"Where is the phone I gave you?"

"I lost that muthafucka running. You got me shot at, asshole. Now where do you want me to take this damn kid, man?"

"Did you forget already? I told you where I needed you to drop him off."

"If I'm asking you, then ain't it obvious I forgot. I swear to god, white folks some dumb asses.

"Hey," the man said. "Who do you think you're talking to?"

"You, muthafucka. Now if you want this baby, you better get ya ass over henh and get him."

"Where are you?"

"I'm still out here in white folks land. Old punk ass dude that brought me here got spooked after those bullets started flying. And you gonna have to add a lil something extra for that shit too."

"Where are you at this very moment?"

"I'm walking down the street and it's cold as an iceberg in a polar bear's pussy out this piece. Now somebody gonna call the cops on me in a minute cause I damn sure don't fit in 'round here. Now if you don't meet me somewhere, then I'mma drop his lil' ass off at the gas station and keep it moving, ya hear. I ain't going to jail for no five hundred dollars, man."

"Five hundred? I only owe you two hundred."

"Yeah that was fine until I got shot at. I'm…wait a minute. I'm about to turn onto this big street. Hold on; let me see if I can see a sign…"

Urban whispered the words, *Ashford Dunwoody*.

"Ashford Dunbuddy or something. I can't see that good without my glasses. I see a BP station right up here on the left. That's where I'll be and I ain't gonna stay here all day, playa. I'm already pissed off."

"Okay, great, calm down. I'll have someone there in fifteen minutes," the voice said and then the phone went dead.

Priest looked at Urban and nodded. He placed his large hands together and applauded. "Bravo. You're wasting a talent out in these streets, man. You're a professional liar."

"Hey. I was acting, fool. Not lying. I don't lie," Allen said. "I ain't scared of your ass, Priest. You got a li'l advantage on me now 'cause I'm on them narcotics, but I promise you that I will get in shape and beat yo mutha-fuckin ass."

"Shut up!" Priest turned his attention to Urban. "Urban, go and grab me a baby's blanket and a pillow."

Urban went inside to retrieve the items and returned immediately.

"Now, here is your baby," Urban said, handing the blanket to Allen.

"Man, is you serious?" Allen asked.

Priest grabbed the crow bar again and gave Allen a look that answered his question.

"I guess you is," Allen said.

"You wanna ride with me or do you wanna hang tight?" Priest asked Urban.

"I'm riding," Urban said.

"Cool. We're going to need to take your car. If they see mine, they might get spooked and leave."

Urban went back into the house and returned with the keys to his week-end ride, the Porsche 911 convertible.

"Boy, you're the wealthiest trash man I know," Priest said, walking around to the passenger side.

"Good investments," Urban said with a wink.

"Where in the world am I gonna sit?"

Urban pulled his driver seat back and Allen squeezed into the seat that couldn't hold anything larger than a golf bag.

"Why even bother with a back seat if it's gone be this damn small?" Allen said.

"I want you to take a damn bath as soon as you get to wherever you call home," Priest said, rolling his window down.

Urban turned the ignition and the powerful sports car roared to life.

They made it out of the subdivision, crossed Ashford Dunwoody Boulevard and spotted the BP gas station. Priest instructed Urban to park. They let Allen out and watched as he walked across the street. Ironically, Allen stopped at the same store where Jamillah had taken her snack break.

He didn't go inside. He stood on the walkway in front of the store, get-ting strange looks from the locals. He was tired of the nosey wealthy folks who obviously wanted to know what fool would allow their baby to be in the presence of such a haggard-looking man. He walked over by the phone booths and paced back and forth. A police cruiser pulled into the store's parking lot and an officer got out. He appeared to be checking Allen out, but quickly lost interest and walked into the store. He came out, gave Allen another look, but jumped into his car and drove off.

"That boy missed his calling. He could've been a really good actor," Priest said.

"Yeah," Urban said, focused on the task at hand.

It didn't take long before a car pulled up in front of Allen. He was holding out his hand and shaking his head.

"Punch it," Priest said. "Get in front of him and try to box him in."

"Got ya," Urban said as he slammed the gas. Zero to sixty in four-point-three seconds never seemed sweeter.

Allen stood on the sidewalk by the store and watched as Urban shot in front of the Crown Victoria like a bat out of hell.

Priest jumped out with his gun drawn. "Outta the car," he ordered the driver.

A young Caucasian male with purple spiked hair, an earring pierced through his nose, and a million and one tattoos all over his body, eased out of the car with his hands held high.

"What's the problem, sir?" the youngster said with a calmness that said this wasn't his first rodeo with the police.

"Turn around and place your hands on the car," Priest said without showing a badge. He patted the youngster down and removed a small-caliber pistol from his waistband.

"Do you have a permit to carry a concealed weapon, Spike?"

"Nope." Spike was still as calm as a politician. "Didn't know I needed one."

"Hey, man," Allen called out. "Can I get out of here?"

"Yeah," Priest said as he searched the tattooed man.

"What's up, man, with that bread?" Allen said, rubbing his thumb and index finger together.

Urban reached into his pocket and peeled off a few hundred dollar bills. He walked over to Allen and handed him the cash.

"Thanks, white boy. And I'm sorry 'bout that night I almost killed yo' ass. You an a'ight dude. I shouldn't whipped you like that."

"Don't mention it," Urban said. "Just stay out of my house."

"You ain't got to worry about that," Allen said, counting his money. A big smile eased over his face as he counted his money.

Priest placed the handcuffed, spike-haired guy in the front seat of the Crown Vic and walked around to the driver's side.

"Are you still in?"

"Yeah," Urban said.

"Cool. Then I need for you to follow me."

"Wait a minute," Allen said. "How the hell am I spose to get back to the hood?"

PART
III

25

Michael Benedict was a ball of nerves. His mouth was as dry as sandpaper and he couldn't stop his hands from shaking. Normally the church was a place where he could find peace and tranquility, but today the house of worship only brought him despair and doom. Ever since Nickali had killed the man in that abandoned house a little over a month ago, he hadn't been able to get any rest. His conscience was eating him alive. His nights were haunted by gunshots, brain fragments and fruitless pleas for mercy. He also found himself wiping away imaginary blood stains from his shirt on a constant basis, just as he was doing now. He couldn't stop pacing the floor of his small, one-bedroom apartment for fear of a life-changing knock on his door where he would find two hulking police officers who would take him away to a high-level penitentiary.

The thought alone caused him to wince. He couldn't imagine spending the rest of his life in a cage with the worst people this world had to offer. He wasn't that kind of man; he was a college graduate, a Christian and he had a good heart. That normally wasn't the prototype for a hardened criminal. So how in the world did he end up in the position he was in now? The question wracked his brain over and over again. All he had done was join a church and become its youth minister. The next thing he knew, he was riding around one of Atlanta's poorest neighborhoods looking in crackhouses.

Michael summoned the courage to walk down the long church aisle, past the pulpit and through a back door to the pastor's office. He knocked on the door, even though it was slightly ajar.

"Michael," Reverend Perry said as he swiveled around in his high-back leather chair and placed a paper that he was reading down on his desk.

"Reverend Perry, I didn't do anything. I swear to you on my mother's grave," Michael said as he rushed over to the man as if he were pleading with Christ Himself. He closed his eyes and made an imaginary cross with his fingers over his chest. "I did what you asked me to do and went with Nickali. I was told that we were going to pick up a baby and that he was going to be placed into a nice home; that's all. I only went along for the sake of the child."

"Calm down, son," Reverend Perry said as he stood and walked around his desk. He placed both of his large hands on Michael's shoulders in a reassuring way. "Now relax and tell me what you're talking about."

Michael's eyes started fluttering, a true sign that his nerves were getting the best of him. "There was a murder. Nickali killed a man when we went looking for that child."

Reverend Perry removed his hands and took a step back from the frail, baby-faced, blond-haired man standing before him. "What did you say?"

Michael couldn't bring himself to repeat his words so he simply nodded his head.

"I sent you men on a simple trip and you guys somehow managed to turn it into a murder. I never said for you to get the baby by any means necessary. I simply asked you guys to pay the lady and pick up the baby. That was it," the reverend said as he walked back behind his desk and took a seat. He nodded for Michael to do the same, but he continued standing.

"I know and I told Nickali that, but he wouldn't listen. He is the one who killed that man, not me. I didn't have a gun. I don't own a gun. I don't even know how to shoot one of those things. I don't even like guns," Michael's voice raised. "When I tried to leave, he pointed his gun at me and asked for the car keys."

Reverend Perry's eyes went from surprise to what appeared to be real concern. "He pointed the gun at you?"

"Yeah, he tried to throw it off as a joke, but there was no doubt in my mind that he would've pulled the trigger. It was like something very evil and sinister came over him. And he burned down a crackhouse. For no reason."

"What?"

"Yeah, said he liked seeing the people outside run like a bunch of roaches. He has serious problems," Michael said in a tone that was just below a yell. "Out of respect for the work you've done, I didn't go to the police. I hope that respect doesn't come back to bite me."

"You did the right thing. I will certainly take care of this," Reverend Perry said.

Michael paced the floor and tried to keep himself from imploding.

Reverend Perry leaned back in his leather chair and placed both index fingers on his temples. He was in deep thought now. Michael wondered what he was thinking about. Could he trust this man? Then all of a sudden, Reverend Perry clapped his hands together and smiled.

"Okay, you go on home. I will take care of Mr. Nickali."

Michael stood on unstable legs. He wasn't sure what to do. After all, he was still an accessory to murder, which, in the eyes of the law, made him a murderer.

"Reverend Perry, what's going to happen to me?"

"Nothing. You'll be fine. The Bible says the poor will always be amongst us. Nickali has obviously yet to learn that." Reverend Perry pointed at his head. "He will be dealt with. As for you, your services are greatly appreciated. And you will be compensated."

"I don't want any money." Michael shook his head vigorously and furrowed his brows. This little confessional hadn't done anything for his nerves. "I want my name out of this. If the police ever find out, I don't want my name mentioned. It's bad enough that I will have to live with the fact that I saw a man's head blown to pieces right in front of me. I can be implicated and convicted. I'm not a murderer!" Michael yelled.

"Lower your voice or you will tell the police on yourself. Don't you worry and you *didn't* have anything to do with this. This is Nickali's mess and I'll make sure he pays the piper for his wicked deeds." Reverend Perry stood, walked over, and placed a hand on Michael's shoulder. "I'm happy you came to me with this. We are not assassins. We are only doing what we feel God would want us to do. Trust me when I say we are doing God's work. This is a war. A war on poverty, but we are starting with the children. That little boy, whom you were supposed to bring to me, had a very wealthy and educated family who would've loved him and given him wonderful opportunities. Opportunities that growing up in the inner city would not have afforded him. What kind of life do you think he would have if he spent his first year on this earth living in and out of crackhouses?"

Michael lowered his head. "Not a very good one and that's why I agreed to go, but I never said I would be a part of a mur…"

"Hey," Reverend Perry interrupted. "I want you to go home and try to get some rest. And I want you to try your best to forget about all of this."

"Nickali needs to be in jail. He is a criminal."

"If your words are true, and I believe they are, you are right. He will get his just due. God has a way of working these things out beyond our comprehension."

"I should've gone to the police," Michael said.

"And if you had gone to the authorities, where would that leave you?"

Michael seemed to understand his predicament and lowered his head. "So he's going to be free to just walk around?"

"We'll take care of it. You go home and get some rest."

"Okay," Michael said before exiting the office and the church.

After Michael left, Reverend Perry pulled out his cell phone and dialed a few numbers. Thirty minutes later, Nickali, the orange-headed murderer himself, was standing in front of the reverend.

"Explain," Reverend Perry said as he rolled a pair of Chinese stress balls between his fingers.

"Explain what?"

"Do I need to spell it out for you?"

The look on the reverend's face told the assassin that he knew exactly what had happened.

"Well, sir, you said we needed to get that baby. You were very adamant about it, too. I told you we could get another baby, but you wanted that one, so I did what I thought was the right thing to do in order to make you happy."

"And you thought the right thing to do was murder someone?" Reverend Perry asked as he rolled the balls faster and faster. "This is bad. Not good, Nickali, not good at all. You have done a very stupid and irresponsible thing. I don't know if you know this, but we are not murderers. This is a sanctuary. A place where we do God's work."

"Sir, in all due respect, you said this was a war. A war on poverty. Did you not?"

"I did."

"Well, you'll have to admit that in every war there are casualties. Consider that nigger a casualty of our war on poverty," Nickali said with a wicked smile. "Besides, nobody cares about those people. I've been checking the police scanners every day, and I haven't heard the slightest peep about a murder—well, not that murder. I made it look like a suicide. So the cops probably figured this guy got tired of getting high and killed himself," Nickali lied.

Reverend Perry stared at this young man with a bit of pity and reverence. He didn't like him but he needed him. To operate in his world, he would have to have a guy like him on his team. An equalizer.

"You know what concerns me even more than your deed itself? Your non-chalance and uncaring attitude about the entire affair," Reverend Perry said for the sake of his own sanity. "We are missionaries, not mercenaries. Are you totally heartless?"

Nickali hunched his shoulders and stared at his fingernails, as if he didn't have a care in the world.

"Where is the girl?" Reverend Perry asked.

"She's gone. She ran off, but I figured we didn't need her anymore. She took us to the house where the baby lives. She said it was her brother, but I don't believe her because the guy's house we went to was white. Either way, brother or not, he didn't seem to want anything to do with her. He wouldn't even let her in his house. Can't say I could blame him though; she stunk to high hell. Niggers!"

"Enough!" Reverend Perry slammed his hand down on his desk. "I've heard about enough out of you. Now I will not have such language used in the house of the Lord."

"Yes, sir," Nickali said halfheartedly.

"I sent you to get a child, but I see no child. The girl is missing, you've taken a life, and Lord knows who could've died in the house you burned down. What do you suppose I do with someone who doesn't follow my directions?"

"Reverend Perry, please calm down. I will take care of this. As a matter of fact, it's being taken care of as we speak. I sent one of my guys over to the white guy's house to get the baby and I'm waiting to hear back from him any minute now. Calm down before you give yourself a heart attack."

"You are in no position to tell me to calm down."

"Okay," Nickali said. "Carry on. I was just trying to get the kid."

"The order on the kid has been canceled."

"All of this for nothing? But I sent my guy to pick him up."

"Well, have him bring him here and I'll take it from there."

"You're the boss."

"Son," Reverend Perry said. "You have placed me in a very precarious situation. Answer me this question. Where was the girl when you decided to kill that man?"

Nickali's eyes registered his thoughts. He had never thought about the crackhead lady being a witness to his criminal deed. His arrogance had never allowed him to even give her human qualities, much less give her the ability to testify in a court of law against him. Who would believe a crackhead? He had been to prison and vowed to never return. Now he was worried.

"She's a witness, son. And if you want to remain free, you had better find her and make sure she joins her friend in the afterlife," Reverend Perry said.

Nickali jumped to his feet with a real sense of purpose.

"What about Michael? He was there, too and I don't trust him," Nickali said as he paused at the door.

Reverend Perry stared at the man in front of him and for the first time in his life, he knew how it felt to be in the presence of the heartless.

"Operation Dark Child brings in a lot of money to this sanctuary. It cannot and will not be compromised," Reverend Perry said.

"And what exactly does that mean?"

"It means," Reverend Perry said in a voice just above a whisper, "you'll have to finish the job."

The orange-headed murderer smiled. "I'll make sure it gets done as quickly and painlessly as possible." Nickali exited the office.

"I'm sure you will." Reverend Perry walked over and closed the door. He returned to his desk chair and plopped down. He reached for his stress balls again. He wasn't a killer, but he wasn't about to allow his conscience to get in the way of the heavy flow of money these kids were bringing in.

He grimaced and threw the balls at the office door; they landed with the bells chiming as they rolled across the hard tile floor. He reached for his Bible. He could always find comfort in the words of the Lord. And after all, he was doing God's work.

26

Jamillah was running again. She picked up her pace as she cut through the wooded area behind the Harmony House Wellness Center and headed up a steep hill. She took a deep breath and clenched her teeth as she forced her legs to propel her slender body forward. Every step was a challenge and her calve muscles felt as if they were tearing into shreds with each push-off. Her lungs were heaving for air, but she kept pushing. After about forty seconds of excruciating and continuous uphill running, she made it to level ground. She stopped running and walked at a brisk pace with her hands held high over her head. Sweat was running into her eyes, but she didn't care; this was a victory. Jamillah turned around, looked back down the hill, and stared right at the Harmony House. *A beautiful facility*, she thought, as she took in the fifteen acres of scenic land that surrounded the building. Green grass was as far as her eyes could see. There were calming, man-made lakes where the ducks were coasting with the current. Some men were out hitting golf balls. She smiled, turned away, and continued running.

Jamillah had forgotten how much she enjoyed the smell of morning dew on a freshly cut lawn. She had a joy in her heart and a sense of purpose in her life that she hadn't felt in years. In the time she had been a resident of Harmony House, she had gained a significant amount of weight, her skin had cleared up dramatically, and after reading a novel called, *Nappily Ever After*, she had cut her hair into a nice, short, curly afro. She felt healthier than she had in years. Her near relapse into the world of crack cocaine had turned out to be one of the best things to ever happen to her. When the security guard had given her the package, she was only going along with the program long enough to buy herself some time until those men who killed Marcus had forgotten all about her. Every waking or sleeping moment she had was spent dreaming of her next high. But after that night, something changed. Her breakthrough was confirmed when Amani decided to take her on a little trip back down memory lane. One day she told Jamillah to come with her. Jamillah thought they were going on a normal store run, but Amani headed straight to Southwest Atlanta, her old stomping grounds. They drove through the neighborhood and, for the first time in years, Jamillah was far enough removed from her former life that she could see exactly how everything looked. It wasn't a pretty sight. As a matter of fact, it was downright sad.

The first person she recognized was Sandy, a girl with whom Jamillah had gotten high and done a number of other ill deeds with on numerous occasions. What she saw surprised and almost shocked the life out of her. Sandy looked like a zombie. She looked like one of those creatures in the old *Thriller* video by Michael Jackson. What was even more amazing was that while she was on the street, Sandy was considered one of the better-looking addicts. The nasty men who cruised through the 'hood late at night seeking to fulfill their deviant sexual urges always wanted her. If she wasn't available, then they would ask for Jamillah. Jamillah looked at the woman and thought, *Damn; I must've been really screwed up if I played second fiddle to that!*

Jamillah saw so many other familiar faces and the all of them seemed to be on a path to nowhere. A part of her wanted to get out of the car and join them as they inhaled the potent smoke into their lungs until the world was a lovely place. But the other side of her wanted no part of that life. Then there was another part of her that wanted to get out of the car and rescue them all. She wanted to tell them how good the Harmony House had been to her and show off her new look. Instead, she stared out the car's passenger window and thanked God for giving her another chance.

Then suddenly her thoughts were challenged. Amani stopped the car, reached over Jamillah and opened the passenger door. "Go ahead," Amani said. "You can smoke all you want, whenever you want."

Jamillah looked at her as if she had lost her mind, but she didn't move.

"What are you talking about?" she asked.

"It's all yours," Amani said with a serious tone. "You're an adult and nobody can make you do anything anymore. So have at it."

Fear kicked into overdrive. Now Jamillah was praying to herself that Amani wouldn't put her out because she wasn't sure if she was strong enough to be out on her own yet.

"I don't want that anymore," she heard herself say. "I want the life I have right now. I can't have that out there. My parents will never look down from heaven and see me like that again."

Amani smiled and stared at Jamillah.

"What?" Jamillah asked.

"Well, close the door then. It's cold out there," Amani said as they both chuckled.

Jamillah closed her eyes and let out a long breath.

"I'm proud of you. And you'll see, it's not that hard. You have to commit to being a better person every day. One day at a time."

On the ride back to Harmony House, Jamillah said a silent prayer, thanking God for giving her yet another chance. She thanked Him for Officer Juan Vargas. She thanked Him for not forgetting about her and allowing her another shot at life, but most of all, she thanked Him for her brother, Urban. She needed that tough love that he was providing. So many times she had played on his love and taken advantage of his kindness. Urban thought he was helping, but she wasn't interested in any help, just a big heart who would allow her one more high. But getting over on Urban always bothered her long after her high had worn off.

Jamillah ran along the sidewalk and passed businesses, gas stations, and restaurants. She saw all kinds of people out and about living their lives. It gave her so much joy that no one paid her any attention. She didn't receive a single strange look. It was a far cry from her experience on the day she ran out of Urban's neighborhood and everyone who passed her looked at her as if she were the walking dead. Now they looked at her as if she was one of them, just another productive member of society. She fit in.

Jamillah turned around and headed back down the Harmony Hill hiking trail toward the facility. She looked at her watch and saw that her run had been completed in thirty-seven minutes. She had knocked off four minutes from last week. She was slowly but surely getting back to her old self.

"Good morning, pretty lady," said Jeffery, the security guard.

"Good morning," Jamillah said with an easy smile.

"You are looking good, girl," Jeffery flirted. "And if those legs get any finer, I'm getting fired because I'm going to have to ask you out on a date."

Jamillah smiled and kept on walking. She had forgotten how good a compliment could make you feel, even if this latest one came from an overweight, elderly security guard who only had two teeth and couldn't stop smiling.

She walked into the front doors of her dorm and spoke to the receptionist. "Good morning, Sasha."

"Hello there, Ms. Doe."

"It's Jamillah."

Jamillah had been Ms. Doe for so long that she had gotten accustomed to being called by the name commonly used for the nameless.

"Oh, that's a pretty name," Sasha said.

"Thanks."

Jamillah headed back to her room where she was looking forward to a long, hot shower. She walked into the room and the air conditioning cooled her down immediately. She removed her work-out clothes and stood naked in front of the mirror. For the first time in the last ten years, she smiled at the reflection staring back at her. She hopped into the shower and was out in about ten minutes. She applied lotion to her legs, arms, and back. Then she threw on a pair of lounging pants and a tank top with glittery writing.

There was a knock on her door.

Jamillah walked over and asked who it was. It was one of the nurses telling her she had a visitor in the visitation room. She also said it was a police officer. Her heart started to race a million beats per second. Questions attacked her brain demanding answers.

What do they want?

Am I going to jail?

The baby sale was a set-up.

Why did I do that?

The questions wouldn't stop, but she didn't have any answers. Something told her that this day would come. She dropped her head. This good feeling thing was too good to be true. It was time to pay for all of the wrong she had done. She reached out, unlocked the door and walked out to meet her fate.

27

Urban followed Priest onto Interstate 20 and they headed west. They merged onto Interstate 85, headed north through downtown Atlanta, and then eased over to Interstate 75 and continued north for about fifty miles. They exited onto a country road without an exit sign. Urban wondered where Priest was going, but he continued to follow him. They made a few twists and turns between trees where there appeared to be nothing. But after they cleared the brush, a new road appeared. Then they were on a long trail with nothing on either side of them but cows and land for them to graze.

The longer they drove, the more Urban questioned whether he should've gotten involved at this level. Maybe he should've told Priest to keep him posted. He pulled out his cell phone to call Sierra, but couldn't even get a roaming signal.

They finally turned off of the long road and onto a very bumpy trail, followed by an even bumpier pathway where they traded in the view of cows for nothing but water. It was as if they were traveling to an island. The Porsche's paint job took a horrible lashing as the branches from the overhanging trees scratched and scraped the once flawless automobile. And the suspension had to be shot to hell.

Urban felt as if he were in another world and period of time. They drove for another half-mile before Priest took a sharp left that could only be found by someone who knew this land well. He pulled in between two big oak trees and stopped. He stuck his hand out of the window and motioned for Urban to park a little farther down.

Priest jumped out of the car and waved Urban over.

"What the hell, man? You got me out here in the boondocks."

Priest laughed. "Does this place look familiar to you?"

"No. Should it?"

"I guess not," Priest said with a shrug of his shoulders.

"Why would this place be familiar to me?"

"This building is an old training facility that the feds shut down, like thirty years ago. We used to call it 'Murderland,' but hell, I guess they couldn't keep on killing folks without somebody finding out. Only ten people on the force even know this place exists."

"Okay," Urban said. He gave Priest a look of bewilderment. "I still don't know why I should know about it."

"Don't sweat it."

"So why are we here?"

"Gotta get some answers. This thing is a whole lot deeper than you might think it is, Urban. Something sinister is going on and I intend to find out what that is."

"What are you thinking?"

"I'm thinking your nephew may be the target of a group of gangsters who sell babies on the black market. Human trafficking. I'm not sure if this is connected to that, but who knows. If it is, then jackpot, but if not, maybe they can help shed some light onto it."

"So what's next? What are we doing out here?" Urban asked.

"I'm going to need your help on a few things. It's not very pleasant, but it's effective," Priest said casually.

"Okay. What do you need me to do?"

"Ever heard of water boarding?" Priest said with a wide grin.

"Can't say that I have," Urban said, shaking his head. "Are we taking the man skiing?"

Priest chuckled. "Not quite, but you'll need to have a strong stomach. I'll tell ya all you need to know," Priest said as if he had some painful plans for the spike-haired guy. "Watch how easily I can break him."

Urban shook his head. He couldn't believe what was happening to his world. One phone call in the middle of the night had turned up a baby, a break-in which could've resulted in a man losing his life, and now what appeared to be some intricate scheme to kidnap babies.

"I need to get in contact with my girl, man, but I can't get any service out in these sticks," Urban said, looking at his phone as if some bars would magically appear.

"Here," Priest said. "This one will work in a damn cave. I'm telling you, bro, you gotta get that Verizon network. That commercial wasn't lying. I find myself looking for that little funny-looking dude to pop out somewhere."

"He might be around here," Urban said as he took the phone.

Priest looked around. "He'd better not be; I would hate to shoot him."

Urban chuckled. "Man, are you always this calm before a torture?"

"Yeah. I really get a kick out of hurting those who make it their business hurting others. It's my purpose," Priest said, spreading out his wide arms. "What can I say? God made me with 'an eye for an eye' mentality."

"Well, I don't like hurting people. It haunts me in my sleep," Urban said. "Killing has taken everything from me. I saw my father kill a man who tried to kill him. Then that man's friends killed both of my parents. And after my sister sat there and witnessed all of that at such a young age, I believe that's the reason she is the way she is. When does it stop?"

"It'll never stop. As a matter of fact, it'll get worse if those who do the killing can go on killing unchecked. But I'll do my best to make sure that they burn in hell because it doesn't bother me one bit to turn their lights out. I sleep like a baby."

Urban wished he felt that way. His mind went back to that fateful night that haunted him in his dreams.

He and Jamillah had just been placed in their third foster home. The first two couldn't deal with them for any more than a month. Jamillah couldn't stop crying and screaming for their parents to come back, so the new families always returned them to Social Services as if they were faulty items purchased at a local store.

Because they were so old, Social Services wouldn't separate them, so they were very hard to place. There weren't many takers for a white kid who thought he was Black with a biracial sister who cried twenty-three hours a day.

The Hares were different. They were the nicest people in the world.

Jamillah even stopped crying and managed an occasional smile. But all that joy changed one night. Urban was fast asleep when he thought he heard his sister scream. It didn't matter how many times she did it, Urban always went to check on her. But this scream was different. Urban jumped up and ran to her bedroom. It was three o'clock in the morning. He pushed open her bedroom door and what he saw caused him to pause. He saw Mr. Hare kneeling down beside Jamillah's bed. At first he thought the old man was praying for her, but then he heard Jamillah.

"Please stop," she whimpered.

"It's time I make you a woman. Don't you wanna be a woman?"

"I don't wanna," Jamillah cried.

"You don't have a choice," the old man said in a forceful tone. "You are my property, little girl. Either do what I say or I'll ship you right back to the orphanage."

Urban left the door and ran to get the gun that Mr. Hare kept in the buffet drawer by the dining room table. It was an old, rusty pistol but it would have to do. He returned to his sister's door. "Leave her alone," Urban said, pointing the pistol at the man that he thought cared for them.

Mr. Hare turned around and stood to his full six-feet. He looked down at Urban. "Boy, you pull a pistol on a man, you'd better be ready to use it," Mr. Hare said.

Urban looked down and saw the old man's pale white and erect penis sticking out of his pajamas. The sight of a grown man's erection, after molesting his little sister, conjured up a rage inside of Urban that he didn't know existed.

"You have about five seconds to get your little nosey behind out of this room or I'mma call them folks who brought you here and have them take you back to the orphanage. And I know you don't want..."

Urban fired the pistol, hitting Mr. Hare in his stomach. The old man fell back onto Jamillah who screamed at the top of her lungs. Jamillah jumped up and ran to her brother.

Mrs. Hare ran to the bedroom and stopped when she saw her husband lying on the child's bed with his penis sticking out of his pajamas. Mr. Hare was clutching his chest as the life slowly flowed out of him.

"My God," Mrs. Hare gasped. "What have you done?"

"He was trying to have sex with my little sister," Urban cried as he stood there with the smoking gun still in his hand.

Mrs. Hare was in her late sixties and she moved as fast as she could to her husband. She looked down at the half naked man and shook her head. She turned to Urban, walked over to him and reached for the pistol. Urban wasn't very trusting at this time. He backed up and pointed the gun at Mrs. Hare.

"No, son," Mrs. Hare said, shaking her head. "I don't blame you. You were only protecting your sister," she said through tears. "My husband is a very sick man. It was time for it to stop," she said as if this little episode had happened too many times before. "I don't blame you one bit, child. Please give me the gun."

"I don't wanna go to jail. I didn't want to hurt him, but I couldn't let him rape my sister. I don't want to go to jail," Urban cried, shaking his head from side to side.

"No, son," Mrs. Hare said. "You have my word."

"I don't trust you," Urban said with the pistol still pointed at the woman who had been nothing less that sweet to him and his sister.

"Look at him," Mrs. Hare said, pointing at Mr. Hare, who was writhing in pain and gasping for his last breath. "A sixty-year-old man half naked in a child's bedroom. Jamillah, run and get the telephone for me, baby."

"No," Urban snapped and Jamillah stopped in her tracks. "Who are you calling?"

"I'm calling a family friend. You can even dial the number and talk to him if that will make you feel better."

"Who is this family friend? And why are you calling him?"

"He's like a son to me. He's a very good man and he will know what to do. I promise you that you won't be in any kind of trouble."

Urban thought about her response as his anxiety kicked into overdrive. He calmed himself, then nodded to Jamillah.

Mrs. Hare called out the digits and Urban dialed them. The man on the other end of the phone was Priest Dupree. Thirty minutes later, Priest came over. Mr. Hare was still breathing when they placed him in the trunk of Priest's car. By the time they arrived at their destination, he was dead. They removed him from the trunk, grabbed a few shovels and buried the man.

Priest used a few of his connections to carry out the cover-up. He took an unclaimed John Doe from the medical examiner's office, had him cremated and Mrs. Hare went along with the funeral as if her husband had died of natural causes. No one was ever the wiser.

Priest walked over and placed a hand on Urban's shoulder. "You had no choice, bro. Some people deserve to die."

"I'm sure, but who are we to make that call?"

"We are men. And sometimes as men we are forced to make tough calls. Would you rather that asshole still be here and your sister end up a mental vegetable because some grown-ass fool decided to use her as his sex toy?"

Urban huffed. "Doesn't seem like I did anything with that one but delay the inevitable. She's still a mental vegetable. Out in those streets and getting worse by the second."

"Maybe, but that's on her. She was an adult when she made those choices. Children have to be protected at all costs. That doesn't guarantee they will all live healthy or successful lives, but it gives them a chance. And that's what you did. Which is why you shouldn't spend a second regretting your actions when that's just what any real man would do."

"Sometimes I wish I would've gone another route. Maybe called the cops or something. Killing isn't an easy thing to get over. No matter the reason."

"Yes, it is. Have you ever killed a roach?"

Urban gave a Priest a look that said, *'you can't be serious.'*

"What? It's no different. The damn bug was fucking up your peace of mind, so it had to go. I don't know why we place more value on human beings than we do any other creature. Folks kill dogs if they bite somebody, but we allow humans to rape, kill, maim and yet some bleeding heart will walk around with a picket sign fighting for his rights. Fuck that. I squash they asses and keep it moving."

Urban shook his head at the man standing in front of him. Priest had the biggest heart of anyone he'd ever met. He was a real-life ghetto Robin Hood. He had paid so many people's gas bills in the winter and electric bills in the summer that it was a wonder he wasn't broke. He had bought so many groceries for hungry families, taken so many kids to the doctor, and visited more schools than he could count. Yet he could be one of the coldest killers this world had ever seen.

"You did what a man was supposed to do, Urban. You didn't go to the cops. His ass would have been out on the streets in two years or less. Then what? I'll tell you what. Back at the same shit with someone else's child. You put his ass where he would never hurt again. And the world is a better place for it. You should never have another sleepless night. As a matter of fact, you should sleep good knowing his old perverted ass isn't trying to screw someone's child. Fuck him. I hope his ass is rotting in hell."

"I wish I was that way, but I'm not. It still bothers me that I took another man's life."

"Correction! Technically you didn't kill him. You shot him. His ass died in the trunk of the car. I've been shot, I ain't dead. So look at it like that if it'll make you feel better. Now get over it and stop being a pussy."

Urban frowned and looked around. Now he remembered where he was. He was standing on the land where he and Priest had buried Mr. Hare.

28

Jethro was onto something. He was finally starting to make some headway into this strange occurrence out at Lucinda Rawlings' place.

He had driven over to the black side of town and started asking questions. No one liked him so residents weren't very cooperative. But once he started threatening them with outstanding warrants and new, trumped-up charges, he started getting some answers. He hated to do that, but he needed to get some information. His first hint of success came when he bumped into Kenny Mays, one of the local thugs. Kenny was a wannabe tough guy and a small-time drug dealer who would never make anything of his life. All of his teeth were gold and he always seemed to wear a colorful doo-rag over his braided hair. The only time he had ever left Elkton was when he spent a few years in the state prison at Reidsville.

"Who assaulted Ms. Rawlings, Kenny?" Jethro asked as he rode beside the man who was riding a bike.

"Wasn't me," Kenny said and started to pedal a little faster.

"I didn't say it was. All I asked you was who beat the woman?"

"I don't know," Kenny said, picking up his pace a little more.

"Do you have any information that may lead me to the person who did?"

"Nope."

"Did you ever get caught up on your child support? What about those traffic tickets? I see the judge done took your license, being that you riding on two wheels instead of four, but those traffic tickets still need to be paid."

"Why you sweating me, Jethro?"

"Just need a little information."

"Well, I don't know nuttin', man. You can't make me know shit, just 'cause you need some shit."

"They say a man who looks a lot like you broke into old man Warren's store. Stole about three thousand dollars' worth of goods. Just over the amount to make it federal. You know them feds don't play around. Ain't no parole with them federal boys, Kenny. So if they give you five years, you do all five and with your record…well," Jethro said, letting his words hang in the air.

Kenny kept pedaling.

"Now, I said it wasn't you, but they got a tape. And hell, you know an all-white jury might be inclined to think all y'all look alike."

Kenny stopped pedaling and slammed on the brakes, causing the bike to slide. He jumped off and glared at Jethro, who only smiled in return.

"They say it was a city boy. Come out henh from Lanna," Kenny said.

"City boy, hunh?" Jethro answered.

"Yeah, they say he tried to steal Keisha's baby, but old Lucinda put a whipping on his ass. He must've not known who he was messing with. That woman can beat most of the men 'round henh when she ain't liquored up."

"Where is Keisha?"

"Don't know. Hear once old Lucinda got to tussling with the old boy, Keisha got the baby and bailed outta there."

Kenny paused and looked away. It was a good thing he was a criminal instead of a poker player. He was holding back.

"Come on," Jethro prodded. "Where is the girl now?"

"Nah, Jethro, I ain't going there, man. You gone have to lock me up. I ain't getting that girl in no trouble."

"Trouble? Why would she be in trouble? She ain't gotta worry 'bout no trouble if she ain't had nuttin' to do with her momma being assaulted."

Kenny frowned at the suggestion. "That's white folks' shit, man. Black folks don't hit our elders. We respectful people by nature."

"Yeah, okay. I've already been informed about black folks and how respectful ya'll is," Jethro said sarcastically. "So where might I be able to locate Ms. Keisha?"

"I ain't saying." Kenny turned around and placed his hands behind his back. "I ain't handing that chile over to no white man. Cop or not. Lock me up."

"Oh, man, turn around."

Kenny turned back around to face him.

"Here's my position. I want the person who assaulted Mrs. Rawlings in jail. I believe some shady business is going on. And I believe that man who broke into Mrs. Rawlings' house is a major player in that shady business. If I can find this fella, then I might be able to help some people. I'm shooting straight with ya, Kenny. All I'm asking is you do the same with me. Now you gonna help me, Kenny? I promise you I won't forget it, and a man in your line of work could use a favor from a man in mine."

Kenny looked at Jethro, searching for signs of lies. He couldn't tell if the lawman was real or full of crap.

"I ain't never lied to you, Kenny," Jethro said, reading the apprehension on the young thug's face.

"You sure you ain't gonna mess with that girl, Jethro?"

"I give you my word."

Kenny looked down; still contemplating whether he should take the word of a white man. That deal had never worked out too well for him in the past.

"Kenny, this is serious business. There are some out there who don't think very much of yo' people. I ain't one of 'em. I believe God made us all the same. I'm only trying get to the bottom of this and help that gurl."

"I'll tell you where she is and I bet' not hear no mention of Kenny May's name, or I swear I'mma get you, Jethro."

"You threatening an officer of the law?"

"Yeah." Kenny's serious look said he meant every word he said.

"Just 'cause I need this information, I'mma let you slide with that one."

"Whatever, but you can bet your bottom dollar that I will be in your face if I hear my name caught up in this shit!"

Jethro was thoroughly offended, but he kept it to himself. He understood where the tough guy was coming from. Being labeled a snitch was the same as a death sentence in the black community.

"Okay, man," Jethro said with his hands in the air. "I told you, you have my word."

"Yeah, that *word* better mean something."

"It's good as gold."

"She over at Maceo's," Kenny said. Then he jumped back on his bicycle and rode off in a different direction.

29

Jamillah walked into the visiting room and her eyes went straight to the man in the police uniform. It took her a minute to recognize him, but once she did, she didn't feel any better.

"Officer Vargas," she said, with a blank expression on her face.

"Oh my. Look at you," he said, smiling from ear to ear. "I wouldn't have recognized you if you hadn't said my name."

Jamillah didn't know what to say, so she just nodded. Her heart was racing. Was the same man whose kindness was responsible for her rehabilitation, waiting to take her to a hell that could possibly be worse than the one she was crawling out of?

"I see your scars have all healed up," he said, looking at her face. "I had no idea there was so much beauty underneath all of that." Officer Vargas stopped. "I'm sorry."

"What can I do for you?" Jamillah said, anxious to get on with whatever was going to be.

"Is there someplace where we can have a little privacy?"

Jamillah searched the man's face. She nodded for him to follow her. She led him to her room. Once he was inside, she left the door open.

Jamillah found it ironic that she was being so cautious now when in her past, she had spent many nights locked up in rooms with men who should be put to death because of their sexual proclivities, yet here she was afraid to be alone with the man who could take credit for saving her life.

Officer Vargas walked in and looked around. He nodded his head, then pointed at a chair in the corner.

"Sure, sure, sure," Jamillah said. "Have a seat." Her nerves were on edge as she took a seat on her bed, directly across from her guest.

"I came by to check on you and to talk to you about your progress."

Yeah, I bet, she thought.

"Do you do this for everyone you refer to rehab?" she asked.

"I've never referred anyone before," he said with a smile. "I don't mean to overstep my boundaries but I was concerned about you so I decided to come and check on you in person."

Jamillah looked at the officer. His eyes were as sincere as they were the day he rescued her from herself. As a street person and an addict, she had gotten very good at reading the kindness in people's eyes. To her and her kind, they were signs of people who were to be victimized. But now she used that same skill to see something different. Was his smoothness a cover to get her to incriminate herself?

"Thanks," Jamillah said, allowing her guard to come down a bit. "It's just that I wasn't expecting you, or anyone else for that matter. Forgive me for being rude."

"No need to apologize. I guess I could've called before I barged in on you. I called to check on you a few times. Asked if you needed anything and they told me you enjoyed working out, so I took the liberty of buying you some clothes and a pair of sneakers to run in." He pointed at the T-shirt that she was wearing.

The shirt was a black tank top with red glittery letters that read, *I'm all that.*

"I thought that one was appropriate," he said with a wide grin.

Jamillah was touched. She looked at the clothes that were hanging in her closet and covered her open mouth. "You did that?" She thought Amani had purchased the clothes.

"I did," Officer Vargas said.

"You didn't have to do that."

"I know, but I wanted to," he said. "After two weeks, you were still here. I felt like you were serious about getting yourself better so I wanted to help."

"That is far too kind."

"Not really. I remembered the shoes you were wearing when I first met you, and I figured you would surely break an ankle if you were out running in those things."

"Hey," Jamillah said, acting offended but she had to laugh herself at the run-down, off-brand sneakers she used to wear. "Those shoes were nice."

Officer Vargas stood and held out his hand. Jamillah stood and reached out her own hand.

"Thank you so much," she said.

Officer Vargas walked to the door, then stopped. He reached into his shirt pocket and removed a business card. "Jamillah, your name came up in the system as a person of interest in a homicide/suicide investigation. It's not my case, so I'm not really interested in the facts other than to give you a heads-up."

There it was. Jamillah's body threatened to collapse right on the spot. Instant stress overcame her.

"Marcus Clarkston. That name sound familiar to you?"

"Oh, my God!" Jamillah said, clutching her heart.

"He was found dead in a City of Atlanta dumpster."

Jamillah closed her eyes at the thought.

"The last person he was seen with was you."

"Marcus," Jamillah said as tears rushed from her eyes. She had been doing very good over the last week at not thinking about Marcus.

"As it stands right now, you're only wanted for questioning, but this is something that you must take care of." Officer Vargas handed Jamillah the card. "This is my sister. She's an attorney. I suggest you call her, or at least get one of your own."

"Why didn't you turn me in?"

"Like I said, I'm not working the case. I browse the system from time to time and came across your name."

"But you know where I am. You are the only one who knows where I am. So why aren't you taking me in?"

"Because I have the gift of discernment and I believe that you are on the right path. However, you gotta get this taken care of," he said.

"Marcus was my friend. Some white men killed him. They tried to kill me, too."

Officer Vargas frowned. "Do you know the men?"

"No, I don't."

Jamillah hadn't thought of a way to explain what the white men were looking for so she felt it was best to claim ignorance.

"Give my sister a call. She does a lot of pro bono work so she might be perfect for you. Tell her everything and she'll take good care of you."

Jamillah was so overwhelmed she couldn't even speak. She couldn't remember anyone ever being that kind to her.

Officer Vargas nodded his head. Jamillah wanted to hug the man, but he didn't give her the opportunity. He nodded at her and walked out of the room.

Jamillah stood at the door and closed it. She walked back over to her bed. She sat down and thought about her next move. Then the tears came back as she realized there was no next move.

30

Urban watched as Priest walked over to a closet, opened it and removed his very own little torture kit. He had a rope, tape and some five gallon bottles of water. He walked over to their captive and tied one end of a rope around the spike-haired guy's legs. He then threw the other end over a hook in the ceiling and pulled hard until the skinny guy flew upside down. He was now hanging upside down yet still maintaining his tough guy exterior.

"I have a quick question, man," Urban said. "Why did we have to come all the way out here?"

"Because we don't know who knows what and as of right now, I need information without the parameters of the department. I couldn't do this in a cell," Priest said as he slapped the swinging man across his face. "I have all day. It's only twelve o'clock. I don't have anywhere to be until ten o'clock tonight," Priest said, turning his attention to the suspect. "Do you think you can take these ass whippings for that amount of time?"

"I'm not telling you anything because I don't know anything."

"Oh yes, you do and yes, you will," Priest said as he cut the rope.

The spike-haired guy fell about six feet down onto his head with a big thud. He grimaced in pain and rolled over onto his back with a look of pure shock. "Dude," he said. "What the hell is your problem?"

Priest casually walked over and lifted the guy to his feet. He was a little woozy, but he still had most of his bearing about him.

"Boy, you're all in," Priest said. "I admire your spunk, punk."

"Screw you," Spike said.

"Okay, tough guy," Priest said as he punched the guy in the face, knocking him unconscious. "Urban, help me get this clown up on this table."

Urban hesitated, but eased over and lifted the man up. Priest opened up a cabinet and removed some duct tape. He taped the man down to the table, smacked him a few times to rouse him and once he was up, he asked him one final time.

"Still don't wanna talk?"

"Let me up, you dumb fuck…"

"Dumb? Who's tied to a damn table in the middle of nowhere?" Priest said as he placed a cloth of some sort over the man's face. He then grabbed a big bucket of cold water and poured it on the man's face.

Fear registered in the spike-haired man's face as he struggled to catch his breath.

"He thinks he's drowning," Priest said with a chuckle. "This is the shit that got Bush and Cheney in trouble at Abu Ghraib."

"Okay, okay, okay," the spike-haired guy pleaded.

Priest removed the cloth and the man gasped for air.

"You ready to talk?"

The guy looked at Priest with pure hatred in his eyes. Priest placed the cloth back over his face. "Waittttt," the guy begged, but it was too late.

Priest poured another ice-cold bucket of water over his face. The man's body convulsed as his brain told him he was about to die.

"Are you ready now?" Priest asked as he removed the cloth.

Spike nodded his head furiously, obviously not wanting to take a chance with his life.

"Reverend Perry at Zion Baptist Church in Alpharetta," Spike said through big breaths. "He sent me. He's getting babies from poor people and selling them to rich people."

"What people?"

"All kinds of people. All rich. Overseas, out of state," Spike said. "That's all I know. I'm just a worker."

Priest looked at Urban and smiled. He turned his attention back to Spike.

"Now was that hard? You could've saved yourself a lot of pain if you came clean earlier."

"I just want to go home," Spike said through tears as the tough guy act was gone.

"In due time. I'm going to have to lock you up for a few days. I need to check out your story."

"Please, man, I told you everything I know," Spike pleaded, still scared out of his mind.

"And I appreciate you doing that," Priest said, cutting the tape with a big butcher knife he retrieved from his torture bag. "And you have my word that I will let you go home in a few days, with no charges, if your story pans out. If it doesn't, then I'm going to kill you."

"It's the truth. I promise," Spike said.

"Let's hope so." Priest pulled the man up and tossed him a towel. "Your life depends on it."

31

Urban pushed the button over his rear-view mirror and the large, wrought-iron gate of his subdivision swung open. He pulled in, looked to his left and saw his neighbor, Vincent, giving the security guard a hard time. Urban wondered how long that old man had been out there cussing out the guard, but he kept driving until he made it home. His truck was in the driveway, meaning Sierra was there, and that made him feel better. He had called her once he got into range and asked her to meet him. Then he stopped to pick up the baby from Ms. Patrick.

He hit the garage door and pulled in the Porsche. He walked around to the other side and opened the passenger door. He lifted little William out and headed up the garage steps and into his home.

"Man," Sierra said, reaching for little William. "Are you trying to give me a heart attack? I happen to love you, man," she said as she used her other hand to hug him.

"Hey, baby," Urban said, savoring the embrace. He leaned down and gave her a big kiss on her forehead.

"Hey, little man," Sierra cooed with little William. "Did uncle Urban make you fall out of that chair?"

Urban chuckled, walked over and plopped down on the sofa. He was mentally and physically exhausted. All he wanted to do was relax. Two tortures and the revelation that his sister was involved in some form or fashion with a murder was more than he could handle in one day.

"Your mother called," Sierra said as she sat down beside him. "She seemed to be a little frantic about the police coming over there looking for Jamillah."

"I'll call her back later," he said as he eyed a big hole in his wall. He jumped up and surveyed the damage. "Wow. That's a big hole."

"I saw that. You tried to turn this place into a shooting gallery?"

"I'm glad I didn't hit him. He seemed like a nice guy."

"So nice that he broke into your house and tried to steal your nephew?"

Urban fanned her comment away. "He's a pawn in someone's maniacal little game. If he wasn't on drugs, he could be a pretty good comedian and make himself a good living in the process. As mad as I was at him, I had to fight to keep from laughing. Remember I told you about the guy I had to smack outside the crackhouse when I was looking for Jamillah?"

"Yes," she said, already laughing.

"That was him. What a small world. Then he had the nerve to apologize to me. He said he didn't mean to beat my ass. 'Man, I'm sorry I was about to whip your ass that night,'" Urban said, mocking Allen.

Sierra giggled at the thought.

"Unbelievable," Urban said, still amused by Allen's antics.

"That is hilarious," Sierra said as she placed William in his bassinet and walked over to Urban. She wrapped her arms around him. "And that's why I love you, white boy."

Urban smiled. How he wished he could go back to the days when his only worry was what he and his girl were going to have for dinner or where they would vacation. He rubbed his temples to relieve the stress.

"Do you want me to get you something for your head?"

"Yeah," Urban said with a horny grin.

"Maybe I can take care of that head a little later." Sierra winked and sashayed her hips into the kitchen. "What time does the baby need to eat?"

"Now."

"Well, tell me what to do."

Urban shook his head. "You mean to tell me your motherly instincts don't just kick in?"

"Nope," Sierra said. "I'm allergic to stretch marks so God gave those instincts to someone who could benefit from them."

"He has a bottle in the refrigerator. Put it in the warmer until it beeps."

Urban took advantage of the rare moment alone and closed his eyes. He thought about the events of the day and how his life had changed in the blink of eye. He looked around his opulent home, heard his woman fiddling around in the kitchen, heard his nephew cry for his food, and thanked God for all his blessings. Now all he needed to do was find his sister and get to the bottom of what had her popping up on police radars.

Sierra walked back into the living room with the baby's bottle, a glass of water, and a bottle of Advil.

"Ohhhh," Urban said. "You're a mind reader. Thanks, love."

"You got it," Sierra said. "I'm going to feed the baby and put him down. Do you need anything?"

"A little peace and quiet."

The doorbell rang.

"Looks like that's not going to happen," Sierra said as she walked to the door and peeped through the tiny hole. "It's the guy from next door."

"Oh, God. Leave it. I need to make love to my woman before she leaves me again."

"If I wasn't reading one of those Zane novels earlier, I might have something smart to say to you right now," Sierra said as she walked away from the door. "But I was, so I'll keep my mouth shut until my body is satisfied."

"Thank goodness for literacy," Urban said with a smile as he stood and headed to his bedroom.

32

Jamillah packed up her belongings and headed for the door. She turned and looked back at the room she had called home for the last eight weeks. Lots of good had come from this place and she was determined never to go back to where she had been before her time here. It was like she was born again. She blew a kiss at the room, opened the door, and walked out.

She went to the front desk and asked the receptionist to call Amani.

"Are you leaving us, Jamillah?" Sandy, the receptionist, said as she paged Amani.

"Yes, I don't want to, but I need to move on," Jamillah said, wiping a tear away.

"You still have another two weeks."

"I know, but it's time," Jamillah said as she walked over and looked out the window. It was raining pretty hard and all she really wanted to do was cuddle up with a good book and enjoy the sound of the water hitting the roof. But Officer Vargas's visit was a warning; a sign that it was time for her to leave.

Amani walked out into the lobby and stopped when she saw Jamillah standing with her packed bag. She placed her hands on her hips. "What's this all about?"

"Hey," Jamillah said, easing her way over to Amani. She rubbed her sweaty palms together. Telling the woman who had played such a major part in her recovery that she was heading out wasn't going to be easy.

"Where are you going?" Amani asked.

"I have to leave."

"Okay," Amani said. "But where are you going?"

"I don't know, but I can't stay here any longer."

"Did you call your brother?"

"No. And I'm sure he wouldn't accept my call even if I did. He hates me," she said as she dropped her head. She hated that her relationship with Urban was irrevocably broken.

"Okay, Jamillah," Amani said as she walked over to a set of chairs. She sat down and waited for Jamillah to do the same. "Talk to me."

"The less you know, the better, but I will get it all straightened out, and when I do, I'm going to come back here and take you to lunch."

Amani nodded her head and smiled. It was obvious that Jamillah wasn't going to share too much information and Amani didn't want to pry so hard she pushed her away.

"Do you need anything?" she asked.

"I do," Jamillah said. "A ride."

"To where?"

"A hotel for now. I can pay you."

"Girl, hush," Amani said, fanning her off. "Let me get my bag. I'll sign out a little early tonight."

Jamillah went to the receptionist and filled out her paperwork to check out. They gave her an envelope which contained the money Urban had given her. She had almost one thousand dollars in her possession and she didn't give one thought to spending it on crack. She smiled to herself at her growth.

"Thanks," Jamillah said.

"Jamillah, you take care of yourself, honey," Sandy said. "And please come back to see us. I can honestly say you were a pleasure to work with."

"Thank you and I will definitely come back," Jamillah said, reaching out and giving Sandy a hug. "I promise."

Amani stood by the door and waited for her to finish her good-byes.

Jamillah paused and gave the facility one last look. She had both fond and not so fond memories of the place. She looked at the table where she played cards with some of the other patients. There was the big television where she watched reruns of *American Idol* and laughed until she couldn't laugh any more at the wannabe stars. She looked back at Sandy and waved.

"One day at a time," Sandy said. "Keep that in mind. You can do it."

Jamillah nodded and walked out of the place.

Amani and Jamillah ran outside the facility and tried to dodge the pelting raindrops as they made it to Amani's Honda Accord.

"Geez," Amani said as she jumped behind the steering wheel. "I'm soaked."

"This is great weather to run in," Jamillah said.

"Girl, you'll run in a blizzard. You need to join a track team and make you some money."

"I wish."

"Don't wish, do it. Stop telling yourself no. let somebody else tell you no and then still find a way to make it happen."

Jamillah smiled and wrapped herself in the seat belt. She looked out of the window and wondered where her life was headed. She took a deep breath and exhaled. There was a nervous energy bouncing around in her stomach, but there was also a calmness in her brain telling her that she was going to be okay.

Before she knew it, Amani had made a few turns and was driving down a residential street that couldn't have been any more than five miles from Harmony House.

"You can hang with me until you decide what you want to do. I don't want you up in a lonely hotel."

"I don't want to impose," Jamillah said. She was hesitant to get Amani caught up in her foolishness, but she really didn't want to be alone.

"Nonsense." Amani pushed a button that raised a wood sheeted garage door to a cute little bungalow at the end of a cul-de-sac.

They got out of the car and Jamillah stood there staring outside at the downpour. "I love the rain. I don't know why, but I do."

"Well, come on in. I have a sun room and you can see it without catching a cold."

Jamillah walked into the small, yet tastefully decorated home. Hardwood floors were throughout the house. Contemporary, yet comfortable looking, furniture sat in all the right places. Eclectic artwork adorned the walls, and a roaring fireplace made it all seem so perfect.

"This is right off of HGTV, girl," Jamillah said, looking around the place in awe.

"Girl, you know that's my favorite channel. That Candice Olson is going to send me to the poor house. Make yourself at home," Amani said as she disappeared into a back room.

"I'm so jealous," Jamillah said, eyeing every detail of the home.

"Don't be. You can have one, too. And you will."

Jamillah walked over to a custom-made bookcase and perused the shelves. There were so many books. She could see herself curled up on a chair with a blanket as she devoured each and every one of them. She had always been a voracious reader, even when she was strung out in the streets. She couldn't get over how nice Amani's house was. It was funny how when she was living on the streets, her idea of nice was four walls and a floor, but now she wouldn't be caught dead in some of the places she used to feel lucky to call home.

Jamillah stopped when she noticed the same handsome little brown skinned boy in about six or seven different picture frames. The pictures chronicled his growth through different stages and different events. There was a little league baseball photo taken when he looked to be about about five years old, a football one when he was a little older and a few elementary school shots.

"I put your bag in the guest room. Now I can't stand being soaked with rainwater. I feel dirty, so I'm going to get in the bathtub. I need bubbles. There is a shower in the guest room so feel free to do your thing whenever the mood strikes you."

"Thanks. Who is this handsome young fella?" Jamillah asked.

Amani smiled. "That's my son, Khalil."

Jamillah couldn't hide her surprise. "I didn't know you had a son."

"I do," Amani said, as she picked up a picture. "I miss him so much, but I'll see him for Christmas."

"Where is he?"

"He lives in Philadelphia with his father."

"Is that where you're from?"

"Yep."

"How old is your son?"

"He's ten and going on thirty-six." Amani chuckled. "And even though I miss him dearly, he's definitely at a stage where he needs his father." Amani grabbed a picture of a man and the same little boy, at some kind of sporting event, and handed it to Jamillah. "That's his father, Jermaine."

"Oh, my God. They look exactly alike."

"Yes they do."

"It seems you guys have a good relationship."

"We work it out. Wasn't always that way because Lord knows Jermaine used to be a trouble man. Out there selling drugs, shooting at folks and carrying on. But I can honestly say that being a dad has changed him. He's turned out to be a pretty good dude. He sends me videos almost daily of something or another. Helps ease the pain of not being there."

"Wow," Jamillah said. "We've spent all this time talking about my life; I never really got to learn much about yours."

"We were dealing with some heavy things. My stuff we can get to any old time."

Jamillah nodded her head.

"Well, honey, I need my bubbles," Amani said.

"You know I haven't had a bath, a real bath, in I don't know how long," Jamillah said as she placed the picture back on the shelf. "The center only had showers and before that, washing in a gas station was considered a luxury."

Amani looked at her friend. She had worked so hard to get to where she was and underneath all of that gruff that walked into Harmony House was one beautiful soul. She walked over to Jamillah and looked into her eyes.

"You're free to join me," Amani said with a seductive smile.

Jamillah looked at her friend with a hint of surprise. She could tell the moment she met Amani that the woman was into women. But Amani had never shown the slightest interest in Jamillah, so she never gave her sexual preferences a second thought. But now it was right in her face.

In her past life, she had been with lots of women, but never of her own accord. Every single time, her encounters had involved some man's erotic fantasy and an exchange of money for her services. Out on the streets, sex meant nothing to her. It was a way to get paid.

Amani lifted Jamillah's chin and eased closer. Her lips touched Jamillah's and she slid her tongue into her mouth. Jamillah accepted the advance. They kissed and caressed and held each other close for what seemed like an eternity. Jamillah was surprised to find herself becoming aroused. She didn't realize how much she needed the intimacy. Her body craved more of what she was getting. It was weird, but it felt right.

"Are you okay?" Amani asked as she pulled away and stared into her eyes.

"Yeah," Jamillah said as she followed Amani to her bedroom.

Damn, she thought. *I kissed a girl and I liked it.*

33

Jethro pulled up in front of Maceo's raggedy auto shop and parked his police SUV cruiser. He stepped out of the vehicle and adjusted his gun in its holster.

Lawrence met him before he could enter the building.

"What the hell you want, Jethro?"

"Need to speak to Maceo," Jethro said. "And watch your tone, Lawrence. I don't disrespect you and I would like the same kindness in return."

"Man," Lawrence said, fanning Jethro away. "What you been doing? Watching cops on television? Lord knows you don't do nuttin else round here."

"Where is Maceo?" Jethro asked with as much authority as he could muster.

"He ain't here."

"If you're lying, then I'm taking you to jail."

"I'd like to see you try it."

Jethro gave Lawrence a warning with a pointed finger, then walked right by him and into the shop.

"Do you have a search warrant?" Lawrence asked.

"Why would I need a search warrant to talk? I'm not searching the place," Jethro said.

"I know that fool. I was just seeing if you knew it."

Jethro grunted and walked into the garage. Maceo was leaning under the hood of a car, fiddling around with some hoses.

"Maceo," Jethro said. "Can I talk to you for a spell?"

"Sho thang," Maceo said as he wiped the grease from his hands. The phone rang in the office, which was about ten feet away. "Give me a second; I need to grab that phone."

"No," Jethro said. "I'm afraid the phone call gonna hafta wait."

Maceo stopped and looked at the lawman. "Some kind of problem, Jethro?"

"Yeah," Jethro said with a snarl. "We do have a problem. You lied to me. Where is the girl?"

"I lied to you?! Whatchu talking 'bout, man?"

"You know what I'm talking bout, Maceo. I thought you was gonna shoot straight with me and here you are giving me the run around."

"Why do you want the gurl?"

"'Cause I wanna talk to her,"

"She's grown. You gonna arrest her?"

"Not right this moment, but if that's what it comes to, then I gotta do what I gotta do. Right now, all I wanna do is talk to her."

Maceo looked at Jethro, spit some dip into a can, then nodded his head. "I'll be right back."

Jethro turned to Lawrence, who had taken a seat in the corner in a plastic chair, and pointed at his badge. "You know you lied to an officer of the law. And you know you're going to jail, don't cha?" Jethro said. "Obstruction of justice, lying to an officer of the peace, and I'm sure I can think of a few other things."

"Man," Lawrence said, standing to his feet. "I don't give a damn 'bout yo' investigation, cracker. You crackers get on my damn nerves, always tryna throw ya weight around with black folks."

"I'll tell ya what," Jethro said, nodding his head. "You'll see what weight I can throw around in a few minutes when I put these cuffs on your tail."

"Do it," Lawrence said, as he got into a fighter's stance. "And I'll knock some of the stupid outta yo ass."

Jethro walked over and did some kind of chop to Lawrence's neck, causing the man to fall over holding his neck. "I learned that watching *Cops*," Jethro said as he placed Lawrence's hands behind his back while the man gasped for air. He cuffed him and sat him back down in the plastic chair. "Not one word outta you and I may cut you loose, but if you open your mouth one time, I'm locking you up for seventy-two hours."

"Hey!" Maceo yelled when he walked back into the garage and saw Jethro standing crouched over Lawrence. "Whatchu doing, Jethro?"

"My job," he said, but his attention was on Keisha.

Keisha Rawlings was a pretty, brown-skinned girl with sad eyes. She stood in the doorway of the shop's office, looking at the lawman and holding a very small baby in her arms.

"How you doing, Keisha?"

"I'm fine."

"I need to talk to you for a spell. Is that a'ight with you?"

"Yessir."

"What can you tell me about what happened at your house? The thing with your momma, Lucinda?"

"I don't know," Keisha said, shaking her head. "I'm still tryna figure it out. Some man broke in and he was trying to take my baby. Momma woke up and caught him. Then they got to fighting and Momma was getting the best of him, so he pulled out a gun. Momma still fought him though. She ain't care. She went buck wild on him so he hit her with his gun. I wasn't going to let him whup up on my Momma, so I jumped on him and bit him. That's when he holla'd and ran outta the trailer."

"I see," Jethro said. "All of your things gone from ya' momma's house. When did you move them? Before or after she was attacked?"

"Before. I just came by the house to get the baby. Momma picked him up from the sitter for me cause I had to take this test to see if I could get into the Air Force. But the sitter called me and told me how drunk she was and so I hurried and finished the test and went to get my baby. That's when I came in and saw that man."

"Why did you move out?"

"Me and Momma been going through it, with her drinking all the time, and I didn't want my baby 'round that. I grew up with it, and I didn't want my baby 'round it, so I packed up and moved over to my boyfriend's house. But then his momma said I couldn't stay there 'cause we ain't married. I didn't wanna stay there anyway." Keisha frowned. "So, Mr. Maceo came and got me and that's why I'm here."

"I see," Jethro said as he gave Maceo an appreciative nod. "Why didn't you call the doctor for your momma? I mean to leave her there after that was kind of mean, don't you think?"

Keisha hunched her shoulders. "I was mad at her for drinking all the time."

"So you have no idea who this fella is, Keisha?" Jethro asked.

"No," Keisha said, shaking her head. "I swear, Mr. Jethro. I ain't lying."

"Okay. I believe you," Jethro said. "But why didn't you come to me?"

Keisha looked down at her baby. "Mr. Jethro, with all due respect, people think you dumb. I couldn't chance my baby with you."

Jethro looked as if he was shot in the heart, but he tried not to show it.

"I'm sorry, Mr. Jethro," Keisha added, after seeing the officer's reaction. "I didn't mean to hurt your feelings. You always been nice to me."

"Thank you, Keisha. I appreciate you saying that."

"Are you gonna catch the person who tried to steal my baby and beat up my momma?"

"I will," Jethro said.

"I don't see why everybody's trying to take my baby from me anyway," Keisha said, looking down at her son. "He's mine and can't nobody make me give him up."

Jethro frowned at the response. "Who is *everybody*?"

"First, Dr. Smith tried to get me to sign him over for adoption the same day I had him. She got real mad at me, too, when I wouldn't sign the papers. Started saying my baby was gonna grow up and be nothing but a burden on society. Then some man came by our trailer and offered me a thousand dollars for me to sign him over to him. Now some man came in trying to steal him. My baby must be real special 'cause everybody trying to get him."

Jethro's mind raced. *Dr. Smith? Why would she try to get Keisha to give her baby up?* he wondered.

"I promise you, if it's the last thing I do, I'm going to find out who did this and who's behind it," Jethro said.

"I hope so," Keisha said with a pretty, bright smile. "If you need to talk to me again, I'll be here until I find someplace else to go. I wanna move to Lanna and go to Georgia State. That's my dream."

"Well, I'm sure you'll make that dream a reality real soon, Keisha," Jethro said. "Just one more thing."

"Sir?"

"Please go and see yo' momma. She may have her issues, and we all do, but she sure loves you. It'll make her feel good, if you would check in on her."

Keisha nodded. "I will. I'll see if Mr. Maceo can run me over there."

Jethro nodded, then looked at Lawrence as if he was trying to decide what to do with him.

"You kiss my ass, Jethro," Lawrence said from his chair in the corner. "Now turn me loose."

Jethro stopped and walked over to Lawrence. "I'll tell you what I will do."

"You better get these gotdamn handcuffs offa me fo' I whip yo' raggedy ass up in henh," Lawrence barked.

Jethro lifted Lawrence out of his chair to his feet. "You are under arrest for possession of a big mouth."

"Maceo," Lawrence called. "Get this fool before I kill him."

Maceo shook his head. "Can't help you with that one, Lawrence. "Jethro gotcha dead to rights with that mouth thing. And when it comes to your mouth, that's got to be a felony."

34

Jethro pulled up in front of the Elkton police headquarters. The small building used to serve as the town's only bank, but it was no longer needed when Bank of America placed a branch inside the local grocery store. The city purchased it and made it a jail. They must have used the blueprint from the one on *The Andy Griffith Show* because it was an exact replica.

Jethro jumped out of the car and walked around to the back seat.

"Come on, Lawrence," Jethro said as he pulled the handcuffed man from the rear seat and closed the door.

"Why you gotta be such a butthole?" Lawrence said. "You just wanna show off. You ain't had to arrest me."

"I didn't wanna do it, but I'm 'bout sick and tired of all the disrespect you keep dishing my way," Jethro said as he walked into the building and led Lawrence over to the antiquated jail cell. "Now I'll let you go if you calm down and apologize."

"Man, you trippin'," Lawrence said as he took a seat on the bed. "I won't be apologizing for telling the truth. You a butthole and a dumbass."

"Good morning, Jethro; good morning, Lawrence," Ethel, the town's dispatcher/secretary/stenographer/counselor and part-time bailiff, said as she played with Sam.

"Good morning," both men said in unison.

"Did I get any calls?" Jethro said.

Ethel didn't bother to respond; she looked at him over her cat eyeglasses and nodded toward a big pile of Sam's poop in the corner.

"Geez, Ethel. Why didn't you take her out? I'm trying to housebreak her."

"I'm not a dog trainer," she said and turned back to the *Regis and Kelly* show.

Jethro cleaned up after his puppy and sat at his desk. He turned on the computer. The town's system was so outdated that most of the information Jethro pulled up was from the Internet. He logged on and did a Google search for missing children. It was useless. The only information he found was about the children who were already reported missing. He needed some inside information on cases in progress. Frustrated, he slammed his hand down on the desk. He picked up the telephone and dialed the hospital.

"I need to speak with Dr. Smith. This is Jethro Watson over at the jail."

"Hold on, Jethro," someone said.

After what seemed like an hour, but was more like ten minutes, another voice finally sounded on the other end.

"Hello," Dr. Smith said. "What can I do for you, Jethro? I'm busy."

"Just wanted to ask you a quick question," he said and waited to see if that was okay.

"Make it snappy. I have patients and they aren't going to get any better while I'm on the phone yapping with you."

"Okay," Jethro said, anxious to get the good doctor back to the business of helping the townsfolk.

"Why did you try to get Keisha Rawlings to give up her baby for adoption?" he said.

There was silence on the other end of the line.

"Excuse me?" Dr. Smith finally said.

"Just wondering. Is that a normal practice?"

Dr. Smith sighed and then went silent again.

"Hello?" Jethro said.

"Yes," she said. "I'm here."

"Is that a policy over at the hospital or something?"

"That child can barely take care of herself. How is she going to provide for a child? I was just being a friend. Or at least trying to be one. It was only a suggestion."

"Okay," Jethro said, nodding his head. "I appreciate your time."

"No problem," Dr. Smith said before hanging up.

Jethro was always uncomfortable around people who were educated in those big fancy schools in those big fancy cities. And Dr. Smith had more pieces of paper from those big schools hanging in her office than anyone he'd ever seen. He placed the phone back in its cradle and scratched his head.

"You racist bastard," Lawrence said, standing at the cell's bars. His eyes were cutting slits into Jethro. "You're a butthole, a dumb ass and now I can add racist to the list."

"Whatchu talking 'bout, Lawrence?"

"How come you couldn't call Maceo? We got a phone over there and it works, too. What you needed to do? Look the black man in our eyes to see if we lying?"

"Lawrence, I ain't no racist and you know it. You just talking crazy as usual."

"'White folks' words okay over the phone, hunh? Why didn't you ask her if she ever asked any of them white gurls who be walking 'round henh swole up if they wanna give they babies up for adoption? How come she only askin' the Blacks? Wonder who in the world could love those little black babies better than they own mommas? This ain't the first time she did it, and with a dumb-ass policeman like you, it won't be the last."

"Whatchu talking 'bout? And whatchu mean this ain't the first?" Jethro inquired as he stood and walked over to the cell.

"Yeah," Lawrence said, nodding his head. "Little Shemika Green had a baby a few months back. Child showed up missing and ain't nobody said nuttin' 'bout it. Won't on no news at six or eleven. Nobody gave a damn."

"From my understanding, she gave that baby up of her own free will," Jethro countered.

"Yeah. 'Free will,' my foot," Lawrence said. "Pay her a lil' visit and see fo' yo'self. Damn gurl was fine in the head; now she crazy as a rabid bedbug. Her conscience tearing her a new asshole 'cause she made a deal with a devil. White man came 'round here and gave her five hunert dollars. Disappeared just as quick as he came."

"If she signed her baby over, then what can I do 'bout that?"

"Man, that gotta be extortion or some kind of damn crime. You can't take advantage of people just cause they po' as a damn roach. Hell, I mean, five hunert dollars seem like a bad deal when you hungry. And hell, once you get to thinking 'bout it, you say," Lawrence wrinkled his nose and rubbed a contemplating finger over his mustache, "You mean to tell me you gonna take this baby. I ain't gotta raise the lil' bastard, and you gonna pay me? Shiiiiit, I'll take it!' But after the money's gone and the good Lord pays you a little visit and won't let you get no peace, then things don't seem so right no mo'. And that's what happened to that gurl."

Jethro scratched his head and turned and walked back over to his desk. He snatched up the telephone. He dialed a few numbers and was connected to the Atlanta City Police Department.

"Ahh, hello," Jethro stammered. He was intimidated again, but this time he forced himself to act like a professional who was working a serious case. "I'm Sheriff Jethro Watson of the Elkton County Police Department and I'm investigating a missing children case down here in Elkton."

"Where?" the person asked.

"Elkton; we are about a hunert miles southwest of Lanna."

"What can I do for you, Sheriff?" the person asked.

"Our systems seemed to be on the fritz," Jethro lied. His system was local only, but he wasn't about to share that with those big city folks and embarrass himself. "I was wondering if I could get some information offa ya NCIC?" He had just found out that the letters stood for National Crime Information System.

"Give me a phone number, a badge number, and your full name, sir."

Jethro gave the woman the information she requested.

"I'll have someone from our missing person's division call you back in an hour or less."

"Thank you."

Lawrence smiled. "Now you acting like a real police officer, Jethro. Now let me outta this damn cell 'fo I tear this raggedy-ass door down."

Jethro jumped up, went over, and unlocked the cell. He backed up to allow Lawrence room to exit.

"You really believe it's someone 'round here buying babies, Lawrence?"

"I don't believe, Jethro, I *know*. And you need to talk with Dr. Smith a little mo'. Who else is always Johnny on the spot when somebody has a baby in this town?"

Jethro scratched his head and wondered why he hadn't thought of that.

"Will you ride over to Shemika Green's house and talk to her with me?"

"Sho," Lawrence said, rubbing his chin. "On one condition."

Jethro knew all of this cooperation was too good to be true. "What?"

"Deputize me, gotdamn it," Lawrence said as he raised his right hand and smiled.

35

Nickali sped down Peachtree Street until he got to Tenth Street. He turned right, then left into the parking lot of the Windsor apartment homes. He stepped out of his car and looked around to see if anyone was watching him. He walked up to the apartment his co-conspirator called home and knocked on the door. He didn't get an answer so he reached for the knob and turned. To his surprise, the door eased open. He removed his pistol and walked inside.

The apartment was a ransacked mess. Clothes were strewn haphazardly throughout the place. Drawers were left open and their contents tossed on the floor. The television was sitting on the floor by the door as if the owner didn't have time to take it. Nickali searched every square inch of the tiny apartment, but Michael Benedict was gone.

Nickali took a deep breath and removed his cell phone from its waist clip. He dialed Reverend Perry's number.

"Yes," the reverend said.

"Bad news. Michael isn't here. He got in the wind."

"Bad news is right," the reverend said. "You'd better find him and you'd better find that girl before they find their way into a police station."

Nickali visualized Michael sitting in a police precinct's back room blabbering on and on about what he had done. Something vile rose in his throat.

"I'm on it," he said with a sense of urgency.

Nickali jogged out of the apartment and back to his car. He gazed up and down the block, hoping to catch a sign of where Michael could've gone. He jumped into his car and looked at his watch. His appetite for destruction needed to be fed. He pulled back onto Peachtree, headed toward I-85

South, and got off on the exit for the Atlanta Aquarium, took a left and headed toward the 'hood. There was a crackhead who needed to die.

Nickali drove around the rough and tumble area called Vine City looking for any sign of the woman with the funny name.

He stopped and asked a skinny woman with a big belly if she had seen her.

"Nope," she said and kept walking.

He asked someone else.

"Nah," a man said and continued moving.

He asked five or six more people with roughly the same results. Even the money he offered didn't conjure up any recollections. It was like she had vanished into the thin air. Then his luck changed. He saw a familiar face walking down the street at a rapid pace.

"Must have some fresh rocks that need smoking," he said to himself as he whipped his car around and headed back in the direction of the man.

"Allen," Nickali said as he pulled up and lowered his window. "Where you rushing off to?"

"Hell, no," Allen said, walking over to the car with a frown on his face. "I need my money, playboy. Pay me," he said with an extended hand.

Nickali shook his head. "Don't try to play slick with me, pal. I know my guy paid you."

"You calling me a liar?" Allen asked as he put on the performance that was worthy of an Oscar. "I don't like being called a liar, man."

"That's exactly what I'm doing," Nickali said, showing the pistol that was sitting on his lap.

"So it's like that?" Allen said as he took a step back.

"Yeah, it's like that."

"You a dirty sunabitch."

"You're one to talk," Nickali said, eyeing the soiled clothes that Allen hadn't changed in the last three weeks.

"You got me up in somebody's house getting shot at," Allen said with way too much animation. "That fool damn near killed me, man. Then…after I get away, I gotta walk in the freezing rain to meet some spike-haired fool who tells me I gotta get the money from you. He lucky he said that after I gave him that damn baby. And now that I see you, you telling me you ain't gonna come through on your end of the deal? Wow! I knew white folks was dirty, but damn."

Nickali looked at Allen with a strange look on his face. He hadn't been able to get in contact with Ryan since he had sent him to pick up the child.

"Where is Jamillah?" Nickali asked.

"I don't know who the hell Jamillah is, and even if I did, I wouldn't tell yo' shady ass a gotdamn thang."

"Who do you think you're talking to, nigga?" Nickali snapped.

"You, nigga!" Allen snapped back. "And you think I give a damn about yo' lil' gun. Get yo' ass outta that car and I'll show you right here and right now that I don't give a futuristic fuck about you or that lil'-ass pea shooter." Allen backed away from the car with his two fists balled and the middle finger extended on both hands.

"Okay, okay," Nickali said, waving him down as if his act was all a joke.

"Okay, my ass," Allen said. "Either give me my damn money or drive yo' simple ass off."

Nickali smiled and reached into his pocket. He was thinking that this crackhead couldn't be smart enough to fool him, so he had to be telling the truth. "Calm down. I was just kidding with you."

"Kid around with kids. I'm grown," Allen barked.

"I'll throw in another hundred if you tell me where I can find the girl," Nickali said, handing Allen two crisp one hundred-dollar bills.

Allen took the money, then slipped it in his pocket. "Money up front. You already showed your colors. I don't trust you as far as I can throw you and I ain't in shape right now to be throwing you no place."

Nickali handed him another Benjamin Franklin. "Now where is she?"

"Lemme use your cell phone," Allen said.

"I don't want your dirty breath on my phone. I'll wait," he said and tossed him two quarters which landed on the ground. "Go use that pay phone over there."

Allen reached down and picked up the quarters. He walked over to the phone booth and fiddled around in his pockets until he found the business card Priest had given him. He didn't like the dirty cop either, but he was certainly a man of his word. Allen had called down to the Fulton County

Police Department and asked the woman who answered the phone if he had any outstanding warrants. He was told there weren't any. Just as Priest had promised, they had simply disappeared.

Allen chatted on the phone for a few minutes, thanked the man who had whipped his butt, then hung up. He walked back over to Nickali's car.

"She'll be here 'round eight tonight. That was her uncle and I told him I had a job for her. So she'll be right here at eight," Allen said, pointing at the spot where he was standing. "I know one thing. She better be okay at nine o'clock or I'll be looking for you by ten," Allen said, just to make his lie seem real.

"Thank you," Nickali said. "Always a pleasure doing business with you."

Allen gave him the finger again and walked off.

36

U rban wore a pair of white slacks made of Italian wool, a white fitted cotton shirt and a navy blue sweater vest. He slipped his feet into a pair of Nike Shox running shoes and placed his golf spikes in a shoe bag for later use.

"Check this out," he said to Sierra with a sly smile. "And let me forewarn you that these will be the hottest things your pretty little eyes have ever seen."

Urban opened up a small box and smiled. Inside the box was a size-one infant golf shoe that matched the pair he had.

"That is completely ridiculous," Sierra said, shaking her head.

Urban had to laugh himself. "I know, but I couldn't help it."

Sierra held up the little SP-8 Tiger Woods edition. "They are kind of fly. How much did they cost?"

"I don't remember, but I can't have my little guy breaking the dress code at the country club."

"You are so far over the top, man."

Urban walked over to the swing that his nephew loved and stopped it. William cried and frowned his little lip at his uncle.

"Don't you go crying, man. Here I am trying to get you fresh and you wanna cry about it. This is golf, little buddy. This is serious business."

"It's too cold to play golf," Sierra said.

"Well, you can stay home," Urban said. "I have a new golf partner now."

"It's definitely too cold for you to have the baby out there."

"Excuses, excuses, excuses. It's supposed to be fifty-five degrees today. That's some good golf weather."

"Yeah for you, but not the baby."

Urban was loving this maternal Sierra.

"Whatever. They have a little daycare place at the country club so you can have my undivided attention while I'm tearing into you."

"You keep dreaming. What was the score the last time we played? That's what I thought."

William laughed with perfect timing. Urban jerked his head toward his nephew. "Oh, you think that's funny? She cheats, man"

Sierra joined in and was interrupted by the ringing telephone. She went to the phone and Urban leaned down to tickle his nephew.

"Hello," Sierra said. "Okay…Hmmm. Just a second. Urban," she said, turning to him. "That's the front gate. The man said Jamillah's here."

Urban stopped and stared at his woman as if she might be joking. He walked over and took the phone. "Hello." After hearing the same announcement, he nodded. "Yeah, yeah, yeah. Send her in."

Urban hung up the phone and looked at his woman. For the first time in forever, he didn't know what to think.

A few minutes later, his doorbell rang.

Urban almost ran to the door. After all that had happened, he had been worried sick about Jamillah and now here she was standing there with two other people. He was so happy to see that she was alive.

Urban flung the door open and snatched his sister inside. He felt her arms as if he was making sure she was real. Then it hit him. She didn't look the same. She was clean; her clothes were new. She was sober and had gained a considerable amount of weight. And her eyes…they were so clear. He stepped back.

"Jamillah," he said, amazed at what he was seeing. "Are you okay?"

"Yes," she said with a smile. She was so happy he didn't turn her away. She had rehearsed her lines, pleading with him to allow her to stay with him until she could work out this mess that her life had become. But his joy had thrown a monkey wrench into her plans. "Hi, Sierra," Jamillah said.

"Hi," Sierra said. "You look great!"

"Thanks. A little time in rehab can work wonders on the body." Jamillah smiled. "This is my friend and mentor, Amani, and our friend, Lia."

"Nice to meet you guys," Urban said, reaching out and shaking all of their hands. "Come on in. Let me get those coats," he said, closing the door.

"Were you guys on the way out?" Jamillah asked.

"Yeah, I was about to go out and whip on Sierra on the golf course, but I can call and cancel the tee time," Urban said. He was jumping for joy inside.

"He got lucky. He's so happy y'all came," Sierra said. "I'll go call and cancel."

"You have a wonderful home," Amani said, looking around in amazement at the intricate moldings, top-of-the-line flooring and overall grandness of the home.

"I never knew anyone lived like this," said Lia, the young girl, looking around in complete awe of the home. "How many people live here?"

Urban smiled. "Two and a half." He pointed at Sierra. "She's the half."

"Wow," Lia said. "This place is bigger than my church."

"Aww, it's nothing," Urban said. "Have a seat. Make yourselves at home. Can I get you guys something to drink; coffee, cappuccino, hot chocolate?"

"No thanks," Jamillah and Amani said but Lia nodded her head.

"I'll take some hot chocolate."

"Coming right up," Urban said. He walked into the open kitchen, pressed a button on a machine, and instantly the hot chocolate appeared. He walked back into the living area and handed it to Lia.

"Jamillah, look at you," Urban said, not taking his eyes off of his sister. "I hope this is not a dream."

Sierra walked out from the master bedroom holding William, who was all decked out in his golf attire.

"Does this little guy look familiar?" Sierra said, handing him to Jamillah. Jamillah smiled and took the boy.

Urban noticed that she didn't really seem all that happy to see him. It was as if he was a stranger to her.

"Look at his little shoes," Amani said. "These have to be the cutest things I've ever seen."

"He's so big," Lia said. "Look at his clothes. Oh, my God."

"His uncle spoils him," Sierra said.

"Uncle." Amani looked at Jamillah.

Jamillah dropped her head. Then she handed the baby over to Lia and stood. "Urban, may I talk to you in private for a minute."

"Sure," Urban said as he led his sister to his study. "You guys excuse us for a moment."

37

Jethro was visibly shaken as he walked out of Shemika Green's home. There was something about seeing a young girl who was a shell of herself due to the horrible injustice done to her that had a devastating effect on him.

"Come on, pull it together, boss man," Lawrence said as he led the lawman down the wooden stairs of the trailer. "I know it's hard to wrap your head around finding out firsthand that yo' people some dirty, low-down bastards, but you can make it better, if you do the right thing."

Jethro got behind the wheel of his patrol SUV and stared straight ahead. He couldn't believe what he had heard. How could this be happening in the year 2009? What he had heard was the equivalent of a real-life, modern-day slave trade. And to make matters worse, it was going on right in his county.

"Crank it up, boss man," Lawrence said, urging Jethro on, after seeing the lawman in a complete daze. "Just think about what the gurl told ya. They snatched the baby from her arms, man. And threatened to lock her up if she said anything. Who does that shit? If you ever want to be the man, now is the time. Time for some respect. You gotta do the right thing."

Jethro didn't respond.

"Do you know what the definition of character is? Doing the right thing when nobody is watching. Well, gotdamn it, I'ma nobody and I'm watching yo' ass. Now, you got one of your own, red-handed. If you do what's right, yo' people ain't gonna like it, but I'll bet you a million dollars to a six pack of beer that they respect it."

Jethro cranked his car and backed out of the dirt driveway. As he placed his car in drive, he looked up and caught Shemika's eyes staring at him through the door. She waved her little hand at him and all he could do was drop his head. She was only fifteen years old and looked even younger.

Jethro drove down the long, winding, clay dirt road until he got to the main street. He looked over at Lawrence before he made the turn that would forever change his life.

If he made a right turn and headed back to the jail, every black person within a hundred-mile radius of Elkton would hate his guts. And once Lawrence finished talking, he was sure that there might even be a riot. But more importantly, they would know within their hearts that he was heartless and just as crooked as his forefathers who turned a blind eye to justice when it came to them. Conversely, if he made a left and headed in the direction of his suspect, all the whites who held the power to make him a poor, powerless man would rise up and ensure he was tarred and feathered in the middle of the town hall.

'There comes a time in every man's life when he must choose between right and wrong. He will either make the choice to do right or the wrong he chose will forever consume him,' his father once said.

Jethro took a deep breath and looked at Lawrence.

"Lawrence," Jethro said, dropping his head. "This is where you'll have to get out. I have to think on this one a minute."

Lawrence's face frowned into a menacing snarl. Instantly, everything good he was feeling about Jethro had evaporated. He was so mad, he was actually tempted to spit on Jethro, but figured that the man sitting across from him wasn't even worth his body waste. Instead of debasing the cowardly man, he simply shook his head.

Reading Lawrence's mind, Jethro spoke, "We just ain't ready for that yet."

"Yeah, but we ready to lock a black man up at the drop of a pin. Always ready for that ain't we, Jethro? You didn't have a problem throwing them cuffs on me and all I did was tell a lie. But I guess me lying to you is more of a threat to the community than a white face stealing black babies and selling them off to God know who. Yeah, old Lawrence's tongue is a mighty sword. You one sorry son of a bitch, Jethro. Don't you ever, ever, ever bring yo' pitiful ass round me no more or I will kill you."

"Now, you gonna watch your mouth when you're talking to an officer..."

"Shut the fuck up, Jethro. And when you get home, I want you to take that damn uniform off and burn it," Lawrence said with a tear falling from his eye as he exited the vehicle. "You ain't fit to wear it and I know you daddy looking down at you with nuttin' but pity."

Jethro stared at Lawrence and couldn't bring himself to respond because he couldn't disagree with the man's assessment of him.

Lawrence stood outside the car as Jethro pulled off and turned right, heading back toward the jail. Lawrence had seen a lot of wrong in his day; especially at the hands of white folks in and around Elkton, but nothing topped what he had just witnessed. He looked up to the sky, but couldn't find the words or even the thoughts to express his grief at being a black man in a small Georgia town. As he was getting ready to walk across the street to the corner store to buy a forty-ounce bottle of Old English malt liquor to help drown away his disappointment, he heard the roar of an engine. Jethro's police cruiser made a U-turn, and with tires squealing, headed in the direction of justice.

Lawrence wasn't sure what was going on, but then he saw Jethro staring straight ahead with a look of determination on his face. Lawrence jumped up and down, pumping his fist as if he had just won a championship game when the joy of righteousness took over his body.

"Now I know I need me a drink," Lawrence said, smiling from ear to ear. "I just witnessed that boy become a man. Go give em hell, Jethro!" he yelled.

Them white folks 'round here gon' hang his ass.

38

Urban sat behind his desk and stared at his sister. He couldn't get over her transformation and he couldn't help but think of his parents looking down on her, smiling.

Jamillah sat in a chair across from her brother with different thoughts running through her head. She knew after she told him the truth, he would return to hating her. She clasped and unclasped her hands while she looked down at the floor. Urban didn't push her; he patiently waited until she was ready to talk.

Jamillah reached out and picked up a framed picture that sat on the corner of Urban's desk of William crawling on the floor, surrounded by stuffed animals. The little guy had a huge gummy smile on his chubby face. It was one of the cutest things she'd ever seen. She couldn't believe how attached he had gotten to the kid in such a short time. There were at least five pictures of the little guy in Urban's study.

"You have gotten pretty attached to him, huh?" she asked, even though she already knew the answer.

"Yes." Urban beamed with pride. "William is the light of my life. He could be the same for you."

"William," Jamillah said, nodding her head. "After Daddy, huh?"

"Couldn't think of a better man to honor."

"Urban," Jamillah said with a deep, stress-relieving sigh. "That's not my baby."

Urban's heart hit the floor. He was hoping he hadn't heard her right. If his ears weren't deceiving him, then this might be the worst news he had ever heard. He had already fallen head over heels for the little fella and couldn't imagine giving him up.

"What?!" he snapped. "Whose baby is it?"

"A friend. She didn't want him. So I tried to help her and took the baby over to Momma's but she…well, she wouldn't help."

"Bullshit!" Urban snapped. "She's still calling over here, trying to get him."

Jamillah shook her head as if Urban just didn't get it.

"What do you mean, she wouldn't help?"

Jamillah looked away. She looked out of the window and saw some grounds-keepers working on Urban's yard. She wished she hadn't come.

"She's not…well…I don't know," Jamillah stammered. "I needed her to do that thing she does."

"What thing?!" Urban snapped.

Jamillah shook her head.

"Jamillah," Urban said, standing and walking around his desk. "I need for you to talk to me."

"I really don't know what's going on, but I do know she's finding these babies homes with rich people. And the people are paying good money, too." Jamillah shook her head. "I was just trying to make the girl some money."

"And you were doing this out of the kindness of your heart?"

"No," Jamillah said. "I'm not going to lie to you. I was trying to get paid, too. You know what I was out there doing, but those days are in the past."

Urban was angry and confused.

Jamillah was scared.

"Okay," Urban said. "Where is William's mother? I need to talk to her. You can't sell babies. That's illegal."

"I know. I know," Jamillah said. "I wish this would've never happened, but I don't regret trying to help my friend. When Momma wouldn't help me, I made my own deal."

"A deal with whom? And how did you find them?"

"I copied all of the numbers off of her caller ID. I kept calling until I got someone who knew what I was talking about. Bad move. Those same people killed my friend, Marcus, and tried to do the same to me," Jamillah said, crying hard now.

Urban didn't know what to think. Was Jamillah telling the truth? Could the sweetest woman he'd known since his mother passed, really be caught up in some black market business? This was all too much for him to digest at one time. He rubbed his temples to ease away the stress. He wanted to jump up and bolt from the room, but he forced himself to remain calm.

"Who killed your friend?" Urban asked as he struggled to take it all in.

"These white men."

"The same ones who brought you over here? The same ones you're saying Momma's doing business with?"

"Yeah." Jamillah nodded.

"And you are sure that Momma's caught up with these guys?"

"I got their number from her phone, Urban. Without her, I don't know these people."

Urban felt as if he was being slugged in his stomach by the world's strongest man.

"And those same people had someone break into my house and try to steal William," Urban said shaking his head. "This is unbelievable."

"I'm sorry, Urban," Jamillah cried.

Urban could see her falling apart and didn't want to chance pushing her away and possibly back to the streets. He waved her off. "Don't worry about it. We'll get this all worked out. You're going to have to talk to the police. You know they're looking for you, don't you?"

"I know."

"Priest is helping me out on this, so we'll get him to take you in."

"I don't want to go to jail. I didn't do anything," Jamillah said, wiping her tears away.

Urban handed her a tissue, walked around his desk and rubbed his sister's neck to comfort her. "Don't you worry about it. I'll get you the best lawyer money can by. If you are telling the truth, then you don't have anything to worry about."

"You promise?" Jamillah said sounding eerily familiar to the little girl who looked up to him with innocent eyes when they were children.

"I promise," he said.

"When you came and took the baby, they got mad and told me they were gonna kill me. So when I came over here and you still wouldn't give him to me, I ran. Then I met this police officer who took me to this place called the Harmony House. That's where I've been all this time."

Urban nodded his head. He was a ball of confusion inside, but what concerned him the most was not having little William around. "I'm proud of you, Jamillah. I really am."

"Thank you."

"Let's get out of here. We need to go and meet with William's mother. Do you think she'll let me adopt him?" Urban asked, anxious to take advantage of an opportunity to keep what was now "his son."

"She's fifteen, poor, and the baby's father was her math teacher. He disappeared and she can't afford to take care of a baby. She's smart and could really make something out of herself but not if she has to spend all of her time taking care of a baby."

"Why didn't she put the baby up for adoption?"

"Because she's adopted and the abuse she suffered in her short fifteen years will make you cry. So she doesn't trust that the state will place her child in good hands."

"So why did she trust you..." Urban said. "Never mind. Let's go."

"This isn't going to be free. I owe her three thousand dollars."

"I'll pay three million, but we're going to do this the right way," Urban said.

"Damn, Urban, you got three million dollars?" Jamillah asked.

Urban smiled and hugged his sister for the first time in years.

"Where does she live?"

"She's right out in the living room."

39

Jethro sat in the waiting room of a busy police department in downtown Atlanta. The Atlanta Fulton County Jail was the real deal—about ten stories of live police work. He had never seen so many high-ranking black people in all of his days.

"Mr. Dupree will be with you in a few minutes," said a black woman, whose insignia indicated she was a captain.

"Thank ya," Jethro said, trying hard to remain calm.

Jethro killed time by thinking about where his life was headed. He thought about the last move he had made and how the power people of Elkton were already screaming for his head. His cell phone was ringing so much that he had to turn it off. He thought about Lucinda Rawlings and as feisty and tough as she was, no one could deny that she loved her daughter just as much as anyone could ever love their child. She proved that by taking on a gunman while armed with only love and courage. He thought about Lawrence and his loud mouth and how that same mouth said the words that made him realize that doing the right thing was more important than doing what was popular. But what most affected him was Shemika Green and how the little girl was almost a complete nutcase. Stuttering and pointing at a picture of her baby, while mouthing the words, 'she gone' over and over and over again. A life destroyed over other people's sick deeds. He would never forget the tears in that little girl's eyes as she told him how Dr. Smith pulled her child from her arms and handed her five hundred dollars. Told her to shut up and to never mention that she even had a baby.

"Priest Dupree." A tall, handsome man who looked like a young Muhammad Ali extended his hand.

"Jethro Watson," he said, standing and shaking the hand.

"Come on back," Priest said as he led Jethro down a long corridor and into a big corner office.

"Wow," Jethro said. "What exactly do you do?"

"Whatever I want," Priest said with a smile.

There was a cork board filled with pictures of black faces. There had to be at least fifty faces on the board.

"Some of those are pictures of mothers whose babies are missing. It's amazing that this kind of thing could go on at this day and age. Many of the faces you see were willing participants in this little scheme."

Jethro stood there flabbergasted at what he was seeing. He walked over and scanned the pictures. He didn't see a picture of Shemika. "We have a guy in the interrogation room now giving statements. We have arrested his boss, who was a pastor at a pretty big church out in Alpharetta and he's singing like a bird. We've been arresting people for the last two days. Funny how these people can commit crimes but when they are caught and find themselves facing serious time, they get religious. So far we have fifteen people in custody. They were calling it 'Operation Dark Child.' Stealing babies and selling them to wealthy families here in the states and abroad."

"Wow!" Jethro said. "I don't know what to say. "I read the paper every day and I haven't read a word about this in the papers."

"Well, the one thing that all of these victims have in common is that they're poor. And the powers that be paid these people to sign over their parental rights, which had them thinking that there was no crime committed at all. So they didn't know they could report it, even though the paper they signed couldn't hold water in a cracker-jack court. These people were poor and uneducated; they simply didn't know any better."

Priest's phone rang. He spoke with someone for a few minutes, and then grabbed his coat.

"Wanna ride," he said. "I got a line on a killer who's knee deep into this Dark Child thing. I'm thinking he may lead us to the puppet master."

"Sure," Jethro said. He couldn't believe what he was witnessing.

"Let me see what you got," Priest said, taking the folder from Jethro as they walked out of his office. He perused the information for a few minutes, then closed the folder. "Good stuff," he said, nodding his head. "Real good stuff. So you have this lady, Dr. Smith, in custody?"

"Yeah," Jethro said, nodding his head. "And the entire town wants my head for it."

"You gotta do the right thing, no matter who you have to arrest."

"Yeah, well, I sure won't have a job when I get back. They stormed the jail and I had to get the governor to stop a damn near riot."

"So you just skipped right over the mayor, hunh," Priest said.

"Yes, 'cause he was out there throwing rocks with the rest of em."

Priest smiled and jerked his head toward the elevator. "That's crazy. Folks don't believe in justice in your town?"

"Yeah, but they believe it's only meant to be used against certain people, if you know what I mean. Yep, racism is still alive and well in Elkton."

"It'll always be that way until someone grows some balls and changes it. Besides, you can find another job. We can always use a good man here in Atlanta."

The thought alone made Jethro want to jump for joy.

They boarded the elevator and made small talk. After exiting the elevator, they headed to the parking garage. Priest walked over to a souped-up Dodge Charger.

"Is this what you guys drive? Geez, I need to move up here," Jethro said.

Priest smiled and jumped inside. "Okay," he said once they were in the vehicle. "This guy broke into a home trying to steal a child. My sources say he's a muscleman for this organization."

"Yeah," Jethro said. "You said you arrested a pastor of a church?"

"Yeah," Priest said. "Some of the biggest crooks in this world operate out of the church. We have a teacher, two doctors, three if we include the one you have in custody, a police officer, a lawyer and a judge in our custody. Crazy what folks will do when money is involved."

They drove out of the underground parking deck and into Atlanta's busy downtown traffic.

"Geez, where are all these people going at eight-thirty at night?"

Priest smiled. "It's always like this, bro."

"This is the big city, for real."

"Yep. I have an undercover waiting at the location. This guy has never seen the woman he's meeting and I believe that he wants to kill her because she's a witness to a murder he committed." Priest looked over. "It might get ugly,.but hopefully it won't. I have a few SWAT members peppered around, just in case he wants to make it happen. You never know what the next minute brings in this business," Priest said.

Jethro nodded as he realized he was in way over his head. They made small talk until Priest pulled up to the location.

Nickali was just pulling up. He drove around the parking lot, and then pulled up sideways to the undercover female officer posing as Jamillah. The officer walked over to Nickali's car and immediately flew back as a gunshot blast sent her flying backward. The SWAT team opened fire on the Russian assassin, and he fell out of the car crawling to a destination he would never reach. Officers rushed him and handcuffed him. He was still alive, but barely.

Priest jumped out of the car, walked over to the man, and picked up the cell phone that was lying on the ground. He walked over to the female undercover and made sure she was okay. Luckily, she was wearing a bulletproof vest under her crackhead wardrobe. Priest spoke with a few more officers before heading back to his car. He noticed he didn't see Jethro. When he got back to the car, he looked in the passenger seat, and saw the lawman ducked down on the floor board.

"You okay?" Priest asked. "It's all over now."

Jethro lifted his head. "Did he kill that woman?"

"Nah," Priest said. "She's good. Had on a vest."

"Geez," Jethro said. "It may be time for me to look for a new line of work."

Priest smiled. "Nah, just takes some getting used to. You're pretty good at this. You have a nose for this. Good instincts and if you're going to be in this line of business, that's all you need."

Jethro smiled. He didn't know if Priest knew it, but his words were the nicest thing anyone had ever said to him.

40

When Urban and Jamillah walked out of his study, no one was around. He could hear the voices in a different part of the house. Sierra was giving Amani and Lia a tour of their home.

Jamillah looked around. "Urban, do you know I haven't been in this house since you moved in? I was only allowed to stand on the doorstep. Why would you treat your sister that way?"

Urban gave her a look that said, don't go there.

"As long as you keep up what you've started, then you're welcome anytime."

"In rehab, I had so much time to think. I started working out again and during my runs, not a day went by that I didn't think about the fact that we haven't been a family since those police officers killed Momma and Daddy. I have had so many nightmares about that night that they don't even scare me anymore."

Urban nodded his head as he had endured those same nightmares.

"Momma and Daddy would be proud of you right now," he said.

"I'm not so sure about that. I have a new set of nightmares now."

"We aren't looking in the past and I want you to do your best to bury that part of your life. Nothing good can come from reliving that phase."

Jamillah smiled and slid an arm around her brother's waist. "Did you really wish I was dead?"

"Yep," Urban said. "I wished you would've killed that addict a long time ago so my little sister could show her face. You're the most important person in this world to me."

Sierra and the others walked into the living room, up from the basement.

"Oh, my God, Jamillah. They have everything in this place—a pool table, real video games; they even have a movie theater down there," Lia said, still holding the baby.

Jamillah looked at Urban. "A theater?"

"It's really a screening room. Only room for ten people," Urban said. "No big deal."

"Wow," Lia said. "I can't believe my baby is living here."

Urban looked at Jamillah, then to Lia. "Lia," he said. "I'm very interested in allowing William to call this his home on a permanent basis."

"William? His name ain't William. It's Shacquan."

"Okay," Urban said as he felt the butterflies in his stomach. "I would love to adopt Shacquan, and raise him as my own."

"I mean that's cool, but Jamillah said…" The young girl looked at Jamillah as if she wasn't sure what the woman had shared with the man. "She said I was gonna get some money. ."

"We can help you out with a little money, but not for Shacquan. He's priceless to me."

"Well, I mean…" Lia looked down at her son with a look only a mother could give her child.

Urban could see the immaturity oozing out of her as she was placed in a peculiar position of making an adult decision, armed with only a child's mind. She looked at her son, who was sleeping peacefully in her arms. "I'm not sure what to do. I mean I want him to live here but I missed him."

Sierra piped in. "You will be more than welcome to come and see him anytime you like."

"But what about me? I mean, I don't even have enough money for food," Lia said as she used her free hand to wipe away her tears. "I don't have nobody. I wanna stay in school but I need to get a job."

"Who do you live with?" Urban asked.

"My grandmomma, but she old and she ain't in her right mind. My momma out there and my daddy got killed when I was two. I don't even remember him. My granddaddy just died and he was the only one who cared about me. Now that he gone, don't nobody care 'bout what's going on with me. I wanna go to school and be a teacher or something."

"Lia," Amani said. "You are looking at three strong black women. And I can assure you that your days of going without are long gone. I don't know you that well, but the little bit of time that I've spent with you has shown me that you have a beautiful spirit."

"I second that," Sierra said.

"I third it," Jamillah said with a smile.

"I fourth it," Urban said. "Even though I'm not a strong black woman, I still stand behind you."

"I really want my son to live in this house. I know he's going to go to a big old private school and live a good life, if he lives here."

"You can go to one, too, if you like," Urban said.

"Who gonna pay for it?"

"Those three strong black women," Urban said with a smile. "But if they come up a little short, then I'll make sure we get you where you need to be."

"Okay," Lia said. "Where do I sign? I mean I'm doing the right thing for my child, right?"

Urban smiled and walked over to Lia. "I believe you are. Now there is one thing that I need to ask you," he said.

"What?" she said.

"May I change his name back to William?"

"I don't care. I guess Shacquan is too ghetto, huh?"

Urban put his forefinger and thumb about a quarter of inch apart. "Just a little bit."

All of them started laughing at the same time.

Urban's cell phone rang and he ran to get it.

"Hello," he said.

Urban listened to what the person on the other end of the line was saying. His cheerful mood went south real quickly as the reality of what he had just heard sunk in.

"Priest, please tell me that you are kidding," he said, placing his head in his hands. "I'll get my attorney on the phone. Thanks, man."

Urban hung up the phone and turned to Jamillah.

"You were right. They just arrested Momma. Priest said she was the head of this whole baby selling deal. Her bail is a million dollars."

EPILOGUE

I sat across from the only mother I'd known since mine was so tragically taken away from me so many years ago. She looked frail and weak. She was ill, dying of cancer, a secret she had kept from everyone. I hated seeing her in those prison hospital gowns, but I had no choice but to deal with it.

"So," I said. "How are you holding up?"

"I'm doing as well as the good Lord would have me do, Urban." She still had a beautiful light in her eyes. "What about you and that cute little boy who calls you Daddy?"

"We're fine. He turned a year old yesterday."

"I'm glad. That's what it was all about. I did what I did and I make no apologies for it. The state don't care nuttin' 'bout those little black babies. They throw 'em in homes headed by people who look at them as just another check. Most of the time that place is worse than the one they left. They warehouse 'em 'til they old enough to get out in the streets and commit crimes. I got tired of seeing that and that's why I did what I did. And I would do it all again 'cause I did it with love."

"But, Momma, did you have to kidnap them?"

"Most of them weren't kidnapped. Most of them I just talked to the girls and they knew they weren't ready to raise no chile. So they gave them to me and I gave them a few dollars to help them." She nodded her head solemnly. "But then they were some of them who looked at babies as play toys. Those the ones I had to take. Those lil' girls were fifteen and sixteen years old. A few of them were fourteen. They don't rap. They think it's cute to have a baby like it's a puppy or something. But that baby grows up and they don't know the first thing about preparing them for life. That's when the state takes over cause they big now and they ain't cute no more. Now they a lil' menace to society. And at the end of the day, who suffers? Everybody. 'Cause those little babies who were so cute are now breaking into houses, stealing, robbing, killing, and raping. And you know what else? This place," she continued, sweeping her arms around the prison, "is filled with people who were failed. If you get a dog and you don't socialize that dog when he's a puppy, when he gets older and you come at him wrong, he's gonna bite cha. And what do we do with the dog?"

"We put him to sleep," I said.

"That's right. We punish the victim. The dog don't know no better. You gotta teach him right from wrong."

"Well, I'm appealing your sentence. You have cooperated fully and there was no need for them to give you twenty years. The crazy thing is, the prosecutor has tracked down all of the kids and only two of the birth parents even wanted their kids back. So that may work in your favor."

Momma hunched her shoulders as if she didn't really care. "I'm already free." She touched her chest, then her head. "Already free. Besides, this place is like an old folks' home."

"Is that right? So you like it here?"

"Ain't saying that I like it, but I'm old. All I do most days is sleep anyways. Now I'm just sleeping in a different bed. Sure ain't my King size, but it ain't all that bad."

"Momma," Urban said, "Why? Why did you do it?"

Momma Winnie sighed, then she smiled. "I already told you."

"Yeah, you told me your personal reason, but why did you go into such detail in court?"

"I'm eighty years old, Urban, and I don't have much time left on this earth. So I believe that God wanted me to expose the state. 'Cause they're in cahoots with the prisons. There is a reason black people make up almost eighty percent of the prison population. We commit more crimes because of babies having babies and don't nobody do nuttin' to step in to stop it. I mean, if white folks were being sent to prison in these epidemic proportions, they would create a whole new law to put a stop to it. But when it's a black face, nobody cares. Why is that? 'Cause black folks don't care. The minute we get a few dollars, we run away and look down at the ones who ain't made it. The ones who stuck in the ghetto get mad and turn that anger into that untrained dog. They rob, steal and kill to get their piece of that good ol'American pie. But that's wrong and that's why they end up in here. So all I was doing was what the state should've been doing a long time ago. They don't care about these children. They don't care if they don't ever make it. And that's why, when the state found out, they locked me up. Can't have somebody messing up their plan for black faces behind these bars, can they?"

I nodded my head. I couldn't help but admire the woman even more.

"What I have started will never stop because the people I work with have good hearts. Now there was some stuff that I heard at the trial that didn't sit too well with me. That Russian boy who tried to hurt Jamillah, but he got what he deserved. And that lil' girl in that town. What was the name of it?"

"Elkton," I said.

"Yeah," she said, "I hate the way they went about that. She sounded like she really loved that baby and it did a number on her. But sometimes doing the right thing is painful. And just because she loved the baby don't mean she was a bit more ready to raise him than she was if she didn't love him."

I sat there and nodded my head. I didn't care what she said, I wasn't going to rest until she was on the other side of that prison wall.

"What are Jamillah and her little girlfriend up to? She came to see me about two weeks ago. Still looking good. I'm so proud of her."

"They're okay," I said. "How do you feel about her dating a woman?"

"Child, love is hard to find so I say find it wherever you can. Speaking of that," she said, looking at me. "You been putting off marrying that pretty Sierra. When you gonna make her an honest woman?"

"Sooner than you think. We talked about a date last night. We are going to Jamaica this summer and making it official."

Momma smiled. "Good for you. She's a good one. I love what she's doing with that lil' girl. What's her name?"

"Lia," I said.

"That's what it's all about. Just to think," she said, shaking her head. "You went from having no kids and free as a bird to having two."

"Lia isn't a kid. She's sixteen and I'll tell you, she's a joy to be around. Straight-A student, ya know."

"All she needed was a chance. And that's why I did what I did. Look at her now and look at her last year. She was headed nowhere fast because she had the misfortune of being born to a poor and ignorant momma who was probably failed by her poor and ignorant momma. And guess what? If they wasn't for people like me, your son, William, would've been running around the ghetto with no future in sight. He was convicted in the womb, but you changed his path. Not saying he's going to be an angel; hell, he still might end up in here, but it's highly unlikely. Whereas before…." She shook her head. "Nine times out of ten, he would be sitting right here."

I couldn't disagree with her. I had seen it so many times.

"Well, Momma, that guard over there is giving me the eye."

"Yeah," she said, looking at the female who was tapping her watch. "I'll see you next week."

I got up and gave Momma a big hug.

Three days later, I received a phone call telling me that Momma had died in her sleep. She had left a controversial, yet powerful, legacy behind.

Over the last few months Priest and Jethro had been staying in touch with each other. Priest counseled the small time lawman on how to handle an angry public.

"Don't give their anger any weight. Ignore them until they fade away," he said.

One day Priest had a bright idea. He decided to let Jethro take all of the credit for bringing down Operation Dark Child. He called his friends in the *Atlanta Journal Constitution* and had them write a glowing story on Jethro complete with a color photo. The title: 'Small Time Lawman with Big Time Heart.' The story was basically one big embellishment of Jethro's involvement, but Priest didn't mind giving him the credit Jethro needed the validation. It was amazing what the article did for Jethro's respect level in the town he'd sworn to serve and protect. The people of Elkton went from hating him to wanting autographs. The attention from the paper brought the town some much needed attention, which Jethro used to ask for some money to update the antiquated computer system and a new patrol car for his new cadet who was coming in.

Priest even decided to take a trip down to the small town to present an award to Sheriff Jethro Watson from the state of Georgia for his exceptional police work in finding missing children. The awards ceremony was filled with Elkton's "Who's Who?" and even a few of the who's not?

"Let me ask you a question, man," Lawrence said to Priest as the ceremonies came to a close. "What did Jethro really do when ya'll started shooting them big guns?"

"He was right there in the mix," Priest said with a smile. "You guys are lucky to have him."

"Man," Lawrence said as he frowned up. He looked at Jethro, who was standing there smiling. "Jethro done turned out be be shit after all."

"Lawrence," Jethro said, "I need to thank you for being you."

"Ain't no other way to be, Jethro. I keeps it real. But you know we ain't done."

"What do you mean?" Jethro asked his partner/nemesis.

"Shemika Geen's baby still missing."

"No," Jethro said. "I took her to get her child, but the girl wouldn't take her. And that was a good thing, because Ms. Green doesn't appear to be mentally capable of caring for a child. I have all of the contact information for the family that's raising the baby and I promised Ms. Green that I will personally drive her to see her child when she wants."

"Well I'll be damned. Y'all done closed the case, huh?" Lawrence said.

"Seems that way," Jethro said.

"Excuse me, sir," Keisha Rawlings said to Priest.

"Yes," he said.

"I wanna move to Lanna so bad. My momma say I ain't gonna be able to find no job, but I finished school and I'm taking some college classes on the computer. I wanted to know if you would help me."

Priest looked at the young girl and saw nothing but desperation and determination written all over her face. He couldn't bring himself to tell her no.

"I'm sure I can help you find something." Keisha smiled from ear to ear.

"Momma!" she yelled at Lucinda who was sitting beside Maceo at a nearby table. "Me and my baby moving to Lanna!"

ABOUT THE AUTHOR

Travis Hunter is an author, songwriter and screenwriter. A veteran of the U.S. Army, he lives in Atlanta and is the founder of the Hearts of Men Foundation, a program that mentors underprivileged children. Visit www.travishunter.com

DARK CHILD

READING GROUP QUESTIONS AND TOPICS FOR DISCUSSION

❑ Hunter starts the story with a jarring contrast between the haves and the have-nots. What barriers did you see throughout the novel that separated the two classes of people?

❑ Urban grew up dealing with the same tragedies as his sister, Jamillah. Why do you think he landed on his feet and prospered while his sister fell on hard times?

❑ Urban is a white man who grew up in a world full of minorities. Do you think his race was a benefit to him, a liability, or none of the above?

❑ What was it about Urban that allowed him to take in the baby with such ease? Was it guilt, a sense of obligation, or something else?

❑ Jamillah had been strung out on drugs for a long time. What do you think made her rehabilitation successful this time?

❑ Priest Dupree is back. Do you like when characters show up from previous novels by the same author?

❑ Priest is a very different kind of police officer. What do you think of his methods of getting to the bottom of the crimes he's investigating?

❑ Jamillah found love with the same sex. Do you believe it was true love or was she simply in a vulnerable place in her life?

❑ Urban was hard on Jamillah, even going so far as to suggest she kill herself. Was he showing her tough love or was he truly tired of her? Do you think he cared if she lived or died?

❑ The basis of the book was the kidnapping of poor children. Do you believe that as human beings we have the right to judge who is fit to raise children?

❑ Lucinda was an interesting character; do you know anyone like her?

❑ Who was your favorite character?

❑ How many Travis Hunter novels have you read?